HOPE'S PRELUDE

The Angelorum Twelve Chronicles

Book 2.5

L.G. O'CONNOR

COLLINS-YOUNG PUBLISHING

Praise for Hope's Prelude

"Unique twist of the angels vs. demons mythology with characters that grab you by the heart." *~Maria V. Snyder, New York Times Bestselling Author*

"At the center of this apocalyptic struggle, L.G. grounds us in a tender love story that humanizes all the rest and gives it an intimate scale that touches the heart… I was truly captured by the love between Hope in her worldly guise as Dr. Sandra Wilson, scientist, and Isa, her…guardian and mate. Their passion is both human and otherworldly, and Isa is one of the most sexy-powerful yet gentle lovers I've ever read. This story can stand alone, but I recommend starting the series from the beginning." *~Alice Orr, Author of A Year of Summer Shadows (The Riverton Road Romantic Suspense Series)*

"Let me begin by saying that this book is not in my preferred genre. That being said, I was very much intrigued by the blurb and the storyline, and I was very pleased with author LG O'Connor's wonderful writing. The author's vivid descriptions and her take on angels versus demons place HOPE'S PRELUDE on my keeper shelf. It was an enjoyable read and I recommend it." *~Kim R., Amazon Reviewer*

"Such an easy read and so suspenseful, I couldn't put it down. An excellent job bringing the other Angelorum books together. It made me even more excited for the next book in the series. Can't wait until it is released!" *~CM, Amazon Reviewer*

"Hope's Prelude will not disappoint fans of the paranormal! The richly layered plot, paired with intricately developed characters and will keep you turning pages and anxious for the next installment!" *~Nate Loves Books*

Epigraph

"The two most important days in your life are the day you are born and the day you find out why."

- Mark Twain (Pen name of Samuel Langhorne Clemens, American Author and Humorist, 1835 – 1910)

Excerpt from the *Book Of Human Angels* – 5 Enoch (Hidden) Translation: Essenes Aramaic papyrus texts scribed in the second century BC

"As it was so spoken, and then written, much time has passed since Michael bound the Watchers, led by Semyaza, to the confines of darkness. Wrath has been meted upon the Nephilim spawn. Their bodies and souls ripped from their being, leaving them shades of darkness to wander the corridors between Hell and Earth without peace."

. . .

"A new breed of Watcher has come, three hundred strong, to live among and as men to understand their strife and to empathize with their pain. Protected now by the children of Uriel, these Watchers will balance the Fallen who have been cast down from Heaven."

. . .

"The forces of darkness unite to battle for their freedom, to reach the key that will deliver them from Judgment Day and remain forever free To acquire their promised reward, the forces of both darkness and light must abide by the laws of balance under the ever vigilant eyes of justice, or be forever vanquished by their enemy."

. . .

"It is with the birth of the First of Holy Twelve that the prophecy begins; it is with the battle that the prophecy ends."

Glossary of Terms and Proper Nouns

(the) Angelorum (pr. n.) All members of the protectorate, consisting of the three hundred descended angels that make up the next generation of Watchers, the Nephilim Guardianship, the human Messenger families, and the human Soul Seekers.

(the) Angelorum Sanctuary (pr. n.) The central headquarters of the three hundred Angelorum Watchers and the Nephilim Guardianship located at an undisclosed underground location in the French countryside.

(the) Angelorum Twelve (pr. n.) The twelve souls who will lead the Angelorum into the final battle against Lucifer, the Morning Star, and his fallen minions, the Dark Ones.

(the) Angelorum Watchers (pr. n.) A group of three hundred angels who approached God after the Great War in Heaven and requested to be sent down to earth after Lucifer and his fallen minions to provide a protectorate to oversee the balance of good and evil as the next generation of Watchers. The request was granted, provided the angels incarnated as humans. However, they remained "awakened," allowing them to retain their original angelic identity, their memories of Heaven, and their past lives with each incarnation. They are physically marked by the lack of a vertical indentation above their lip (philtrum). Also known as the Sanctus Angelorum protectorate or *Defensores Contra Malum.*

Calling (n.) Official request by the Angelorum for acceptance into the Angelorum. For a Soul Seeker within a Trinity, it's the time during which the Center Stone of the Trinity is revealed and the full powers of the Soul Seeker are activated.

Center Stone (n.) Physically, the Center Stone is held in the middle of each Trinity Stone, representing the soul in which the Trinity is tied and in which the mission is centered.

Cloaking (v.) Nephilim power. Hiding behind the veil of invisibility. To hide someone under the veil requires physical contact. Those connected under the veil can see and hear one another but cannot be seen or heard by anyone outside the veil.

Dark Ones (pr. n.) Angels who were cast out of Heaven with Lucifer (the Morning Star) after the Great War in Heaven. Their wings were torn from their bodies so they could never return.

Defensores Contra Malum (pr. n.) Another Latin name for the Sanctus Angelorum protectorate. Translates to the Protectors from Evil and is contained in the hidden scripture, the *Book of Human Angels*.

Demon (n.) Disembodied spirits of Nephilim spawned by Semyaza and the first Watchers. Used as Hunters for the Dark Ones. They appear as a black, inky haze before manifesting into the physical form of a demonic satyr. Members of the Angelorum can feel their presence through the onset of a sudden migraine-like headache and through the taste of tar on the tongue. When they die, they turn to black ash.

Divine Visitation (n.) An interlude between an angel of the Powers and a descended human angel of the Angelorum, resulting in the conception of a Nephilim child.

Enoch (pr. n.) Appears in Genesis, the seventh of the pre-Deluge Patriarchs. Great-grandfather to Noah. Believed to have been taken from Earth to become the angel Metatron. The apocryphal Books of Enoch are attributed to him. Semyaza and the angelic Watchers inhabited Earth during his lifetime, and he bore witness to their sins.

Fallen (pr. n.) See Dark Ones.

(the) Flow (n.) The electromagnetic field surrounding Earth is utilized by the Angelorum for communication and the transmission of healing energy.

Guardian (n.) Nephilim warrior. May or may not be actively assigned to a current Trinity. As part of a Trinity, they have an oath to protect the members of their Trinity.

(the) Guardianship (pr. n.) The Nephilim warriors who provide protection for the Angelorum. Guardians can be assigned to a Trinity to protect a Messenger and a Soul Seeker as they pursue their mission.

Hunter (n.) Trackers working for the Dark Ones who hunt and destroy Soul Seekers and other Angelorum members. Can be either disembodied entities or physical, soulless humans.

Irin (pr. n.) Angels assigned to watch the Watchers and record human history on Earth. Also known as the Archivists. They are the librarians for the Flow.

Libre Homo Angelorum (n.) Translated from Latin as the *Book of Human Angels.* The hidden scripture not contained in the Bible that tells the story of the Watchers of the Angelorum.

Messenger (n.) A human who can communicate directly with the Angelorum Watchers. Messengers have telepathic abilities that are awakened when they are Called to become part of a Trinity. They provide communication and guidance to the Trinity. Messenger traits are inherited through the bloodline of their fathers.

Nephilim (n., plural) **Nephil** (n., singular) Being that is conceived by one of the Angelorum-descended angels in partnership with an angel of the Powers through divine visitation. The child is half-human and half-angel. Angelic characteristics include hidden wings and the ability to fly; telepathic communication with other Nephilim and their Trinity; ability to use the angelic prayers (an example would be the ability to hide behind a veil of invisibility when needed); and ability to use the angelic language (an example would be the ability to speak with other beings or former beings of Heaven). In addition, the Nephilim are born without the ability to procreate and can live for up to five hundred years. A significantly improved version from the evil Nephilim of Genesis, who were created by Semyaza and the disobedient angelic Watchers.

Nephilim class (n.) Every century of Nephilim has a class number. Once a Nephilim reaches one hundred years old, they enter the One Hundred Class, and with each subsequent century, they advance to the next class. The last class is the Four Hundred Class, which is composed of those who turn four hundred years old and whose lifespan ends before they reach five hundred years old.

Powers (pr. n.) The 9th Order of Angels in Heaven. The great warrior angels considered the last defense of Heaven.

The Prophecy (n.) The prediction that a final battle would occur between the Angelorum and the Dark Ones, led by twelve souls who have the power to overcome evil and banish the Fallen into the prison where they belong for the rest of eternity.

Semyaza (pr. n.) Fallen angel of apocryphal Jewish and Christian tradition. Believed to be the leader of the angelic Watchers sent to Earth to watch over man.

Sentinel (n.) One who keeps watch and identifies members of the Angelorum and the Fallen.

Soul Seeker (n.) A human who is bound to the soul of another. When the time is right, the Seeker will be Called to participate in an event involving the bound soul (Center Stone), which holds significance in the balance between good and evil. The Seeker is the part of the Trinity, partnered with a Messenger and a Guardian, with the farthest link to the Angelorum Watchers for the protection of both parties. Seekers can have healing and/or other abilities.

Soul Separator (n.) The angelic sword used to cast out a demon that possesses a living human.

Soulless (n.) A human who relinquishes their soul as food for the Dark Ones. The aura of a soulless human is black and cloudy, the same as a demon. When killed, they turn to black sand.

Sphinx (n.) Ice minions controlled by Emanelech. Creatures who stand guard at the entrance into the first circle of Hell. Conjured in the form of twins, Chaos and Destruction. They can block the Nephilim and Trinity telepathic communication. A force more powerful than Nephilim, yet few in number.

Transporter (n.) Suborder of the Powers, the 9th Order of Angels. A type of angel who transports souls to their final resting ground, be it Heaven or Hell. Another name for a Reaper.

Trinity Pool (n.) A pool of white sand containing the Trinity Stones, which represent each Trinity assigned to a current or future event that could tip the balance of good vs. evil. The Trinity Pool is located in the inner sanctum of the Angelorum Sanctuary. The stones in the pool are alive and continually change as individuals make free will decisions, which can impact the outcome of events. They pulse with colorful light and can speak to those who can hear them. They are the link between Heaven and Earth.

Trinity Stone (n.) A smooth triangular stone with rounded edges, divided into three parts — representing each member of the Trinity — which surround a Center Stone embedded in the middle — representing the soul in which the Soul Seeker is connected and who will be part of an event that will tip the balance of good vs. evil. As free will decisions are made that lock in destinies, secrets are revealed.

Trinity (n.) Three parties joined together by a Center Stone: a Soul Seeker, a Messenger, and a Guardian.

Uriel (pr. n) Archangel and leader of the Powers.

Watchers (pr. n.) Also known as Grigori. Fallen angels who broke their covenant with God by fornicating with human women to create evil half-breed Nephilim and sharing the mysteries they were prohibited from teaching humans. Created Nephilim spawn who were destroyed in the Great Flood referenced in Genesis. The Archangel Michael has bound them for seventy generations in the valleys of Earth until Judgment Day.

PART 1: SAMUEL'S SONG

Chapter 1

SAMUEL
Northern California.

"AHHH!!!!" Samuel let out an ear-splitting scream and shot upright on the lumpy straw mattress. He trembled in the darkness, his nerve endings roaring with pain as if touched by demon-fire.

"It's just a dream," he muttered through panting breaths, drawing in the foul dungeon air. Much like the French fortress of his childhood, the Northern California compound had been his home for nearly a century. He cradled his head, his cheeks blazing against his palms as sweat trickled down the scars on his chest beneath his ragged shirt.

Fever, he thought, the only condition under which he could sweat. Or so he'd been told by one of the many scientists who had experimented on him.

The latest injection must be the culprit. Not that he knew the purpose. The tests were endless. When he wasn't being beaten or left forgotten in his cell, he was used as a lab specimen, and not for the first time.

Still, he'd take this round over the exhaustive studies focused on his reproductive system, which had lasted for nearly two decades. Nothing had since come close to that level of humiliation. Being shackled naked while strangers manipulated his sex organs and probed his orifices with instruments had been soul-crushing.

But the worst affront was being forced into intimate acts for a roomful of academics hiding behind two-way mirrors. He wondered if those tests had a true scientific purpose or were only intended to satisfy some perverse pleasure. If the archdemon imprisoning him had anything to do with it, he might wager on the latter.

Once the scientists realized he couldn't reproduce, he prayed the tests would stop.

They didn't.

Clamping his eyes shut, Samuel tried to still his quaking muscles. The only thing sustaining his spirit was the prophecy of his salvation, burning like a solitary flame lighting his path to freedom. One day, his life would be his own to fulfill his divine purpose. Lives would be saved because he lived, and his captors would pay once he took his place as one of the Holy Twelve chosen to lead the final battle between good and evil.

But over a century and a half of brutality at the hands of the enemy would shake the resolve of even the most faithful. What he would give to feel Marie-Claire's motherly touch on his forehead. Her kindness and love as a child had been a beacon of hope that more than cruelty and duplicity existed in the world.

Now gone over 140 years, Marie-Clare still visited his dreams on days he struggled to keep his faith and contemplated death. She would rekindle his resolve, reminding him of the day she shared the truth and his purpose…

France. 1882.

SAMUEL SAT ON THE LOW, wooden farm table in the prison kitchen as Marie-Claire tended his wounds. The small crackling fire in the hearth did little to chase away the dampness that hung in the air inside the stone-walled fortress. He wrung his hands, wondering what he'd done this time to earn the beating he'd endured.

His father had him dragged from his dungeon room to a torture chamber on the level below, the one with the whipping post. It had been a good day, only twenty lashes, leaving him still able to move under his own power. His skin was aflame as blood ran down his ravaged back to soak the waist of ill-fitting undergarments.

What had caused the beating this time? Could it be his ungainly stature? Only fourteen, he was taller than most full-grown men. Or, his fair hair? That had accounted for more beatings than he could count, to the point that he had begged Marie-Claire to shear him to his bare skull, which only made his father angrier and earned him more beatings.

Marie-Claire silently applied homemade salve, which smelled of rosemary. The pressure from her fingers sent excruciating pain through his jagged flesh and made his eyes water, but he refused to cry and show weakness.

Angry, unintelligible muttering escaped her lips; the only speech she could manage with a fleshy stub in place of what had once been her tongue. Even without words, her bright eyes held warmth and compassion. Without her, he wouldn't have survived. No one lived very long under these conditions, especially the aged, such as Marie-Claire. Fear of losing her consumed him some nights before he fell asleep.

She paused. A deep, wracking rumble from the center of her chest burst forth before she could stifle it with the back of a gnarled hand.

"Marie-Claire?" His pulse quickened. He twisted on the table to look at her, ignoring the biting pain of fusing skin as he shifted. She waved him off and turned away, her gray braid swinging softly on her back as she muffled the worst of the cough.

After she quelled her fit, she returned to work.

By the time her knotted yet nimble fingers applied the last of the salve, Samual's pain had dulled with its cooling effect. Setting down the wooden bowl, she hobbled to the cast-iron stove.

A ladle scraped the bottom of the black caldron, and she returned carrying a small bowl filled with thin gruel and half a potato. She held it out.

His stomach ached from hunger as guilt overwhelmed him; he suspected this was her share of the food. He fought back a lump rising in his throat and accepted her offering.

Nodding, she smiled, her eyes crinkling, and patted him on the side of the head. Then, she motioned him to move to the bench, taking a seat across from him while he ate.

To please her, he used the spoon she provided to savor every drop. It seemed important to her that he acquire manners and be well educated. His father's consort secretly supplied Marie-Claire with books and teaching materials to use with him — all carefully hidden for their late-night lessons. Marie-Claire had taken over for his nurse after he'd been sent to the dungeon at age nine. Her teaching skills were uncanny despite not having a voice.

Maybe she thought using utensils would make him less wretched. Regardless, her kindness and companionship sustained him. He'd do anything to stay in her good favor.

"Samuel, mon cher, *can you hear me?"*

Thunk. The spoon slipped from Samuel's hand onto the wooden table. He stiffened, overtaken with fear that Marie-Claire would be punished for feeding him. He glanced over his shoulder, wincing from the movement, and frowned.

No one was there.

Marie grasped his wrist. *"You can hear me, can't you?"* His gaze locked on hers, but it took him a moment to realize the dulcet voice inside his head was *Marie-Claire.*

He gaped. "Yes," he whispered.

"Not out loud — with your mind. Think what it is that you want to say."

"How are you doing that?" he asked, wondering if she could really hear his thoughts.

Her lips turned up and then flattened. *"There is much to explain now that you are ready, mon cher."* Her rough palm was warm on the back of his hand. *"Many nights I've tried to speak with you thus. Tonight is the first time that you've heeded my call."*

He stared, dumbstruck.

She squeezed his hand and met his gaze. *"We're special, each of us in our own way. You are Nephilim, a child of Uriel. The angelic blood of your father runs through your human veins. As for me, what I am is less important."*

Her words made no sense. *"What?"*

She dropped her hands to her lap. *"Much time will be needed to answer your questions... to explain it all. For now, know that you're not alone, Samuel."*

Heaviness settled in his brow. *"Samuel?"*

A small smile curved her lips. *"Yes, mon cher. That is your given name."*

"Why has my father never used it? He calls me Mongrel or Abomination." Realizing he wasn't nameless as he'd always believed spurred a flutter of warmth in his chest.

"It's the name your mother gave you. The archdemon you call father... is not. You are but a spoil of war. A prisoner who was raised to believe he is demon spawn, while the opposite is true. You are angelic in nature. That's why he despises you and why you're punished. You're an unwelcome reminder of what the Dark Ones lost and will never regain."

Samuel sat frozen. *"How can this be true?"*

"It's only one of many truths." She coughed and pulled her shawl more securely around her shoulders. *"Do you ever wonder why you never feel cold, or why you heal so quickly unless they use the cursed whips like tonight?"*

He'd never given it much thought. *"No."*

She touched his hand again and held it with strong, twisted fingers. *"As Nephilim, you have certain gifts and strengths that, as of yet, are not fully present. You sit on the cusp of manhood. Soon, your body* will awaken in many ways. Your wings will emerge, and with them so shall your power."

Samuel's eyes went wide, and his mind filled with questions. *"Wings?"*

"Yes, mon cher. You will have wings to call on your command. At rest, they shall remain hidden."

For a moment, she reminded him of those prisoners who spoke fantastical and delusional words before they died. Could she be ill?

"You're important, Samuel, and your time will come. Play their game. You're destined for something greater. A time will come when you'll save many lives. When that time comes, you'll know it. Hide your intelligence, and gain their trust to secure your freedom," she said.

Her words slowly sank in, and he gritted his teeth, feeling empowered for the first time in his life. *"But I want revenge."*

"They will pay, but in a way that is more crippling. Patience and a humble façade will be the key to everything. Then you can go home . . . where you belong."

His mouth dried from fear, but tasted of hope. *"I know nothing of a home, except here with you,"* he said, unable to bear the thought of leaving her behind.

"This is nothing but your prison. You have a mother who awaits you and others who will welcome you."

Anger bubbled in his chest, and he bristled. *"If my mother wanted me so badly, why hasn't she come for me?"*

Marie-Claire's warm gaze met his. *"Because you were stolen from her and she thinks you're dead, my sweet boy."*

"What?" It took a moment for him to understand before his eyes welled with the possibility that he *was* wanted. He had always believed the archdemon who claimed to be his "father" — that his mother had reviled and abandoned him. *"What if she dies before I escape?"*

"That, mon cher, I promise, will never happen."

"Are you a seer?" Samuel asked with sudden excitement.

"No, but I carry the message that was meant only for you. Nothing more, nothing less. Be warned, reveal nothing of what I teach you. Your life depends on it."

The heavy wood door flung open, slamming against the rough stone. A guard glared at them. "Time for him to return to his cell, old woman."

Marie-Claire caught Samuel's eye a moment before she dipped her head and rose from the table. She motioned for Samuel to go.

He grabbed his clothes as the guard jerked him to his feet and hauled him to the door.

For once, he didn't fight back.

WITH A DEEP SIGH, Samuel's respiration eased, and the pain subsided. He lay back onto the too-small mattress and curled into a fetal position, hungering for human contact that would never come.

Closing his eyes, he prayed that what Marie-Claire had foretold would happen soon. In the meantime, his only hope for freedom hinged on the same person who could destroy him.

Hours later, keys rattled on the other side of the door and twisted in the lock. Samuel sat up with a start; the fever from the night before was gone.

The door cracked open. Samual raised a hand to block his eyes from the light cutting through the darkness around the hulking twins in the doorway.

Chaos and Destruction.

He couldn't tell one pale, pasty Sphinx from the other. Even at six-foot-seven, Samuel was no match for his watchdogs, who topped seven-feet and outweighed him by at least one hundred pounds. Ten times more powerful than him, they could crush his forearm with a fist. And they had. More than once.

Through several thwarted escape attempts after Marie-Clare died, Samuel learned the hard way that Sphinxes blocked his Nephilim powers, neutralizing his angelic side. Still, he only gave up trying to flee after Achanelech placed an unremovable demonic amulet around his neck that tracked his every movement. Even if he escaped, the amulet would stop his heart when he hit the ground's warded perimeter—something else he'd learned the hard way.

Now, he patiently awaited another path to freedom, which Marie-Claire had promised would come.

The willowy figure of the archdemon's consort, Emanelech, entered between the Sphinx twins, carrying an electric lantern.

"Go," she barked at her two minions. The door clanged shut, and she approached inside the lantern's wide, arching glow.

"*Mon chouchou*," Emanelech said softly, using an endearment she bestowed on him as a child. Though he never understood how "my little cabbage" translated to "her darling" or "her favorite." Then again, she was accustomed to inventing her own rules.

He rose from the pallet and gave her a silent, circumspect stare. They had an unspoken agreement. She would remain his silent patron. The only one he had. In return, he would never reveal their interactions or the gifts she'd given him, and he would help her as she needed.

Though over the years, he'd learned her kindness was sprinkled with indifference and unexplained moments of cruelty. He didn't understand her motivation or affection for him any better now than he had as a child. True, she had protected him on many occasions, while leaving him to suffer at her demon lover's whim on many others.

He fisted his hands and challenged her on a promise she'd made during her last visit. "You said the tests would stop," he said quietly, meeting her eyes and biting back his welling anger.

Giving him a tight smile, she cocked her head, and her pupils shifted from bright blue to black. "A little demanding today, aren't we? Wake up on the wrong side of the pallet?"

He lowered his head to hide his gritted teeth. "Why did you come, Mistress?"

Her voice softened. "To give you good news." She touched his shoulder, leaving an icy, prickling sensation when her fingers retreated. "I have a plan, but I'll need your help. It will guarantee an end to your days as a lab specimen and hopefully yield better accommodations."

He lifted his head, a spark of hope igniting. "What do you need?" Even as he asked, he knew there must be something important in it for her. No doubt the execution of her plan carried a risk of pain and suffering for him.

Her pupils lightened to blue, and her smile took on a mischievous twist. "You'll see." She arched a brow. "In the meantime, I have to pay Acchie a visit upstairs and do some heavy convincing."

Acchie. Her nickname for his self-proclaimed father, Achanelech. The Demon King of Fire. Lieutenant to Lucifer himself.

"Later, pet," she said and blew him an icy kiss. The glow of her lantern headed to the door. "Before I go, did you enjoy my gift?"

He thought of the worn copy of *The DaVinci Code* hidden beneath his pallet. For years after Marie-Claire died, Emanelech had smuggled him books with matches and tapers to read by. Classics when he was young and whatever was current as he got older. Always fiction, anything ranging from thrillers to romance. He suspected they were her castoffs. Either way, they provided one of his only links to the outside world.

"Yes, thank you," he whispered, but the words felt like ground glass on his tongue.

"Good. I'll have Destruction bring a few more books if all goes well upstairs. Ta-ta for now." The door thumped closed behind her, leaving him again draped in darkness.

Chapter 2

EMANELECH

"EM, WHAT'S SO IMPORTANT that it can't wait until my day is done?" Achanelech glared at her from across his heavy wooden desk. The polished sycamore surface was hidden beneath piles of paperwork and his open laptop. His black eyes blazed with a color matching his long, slicked-back hair, and the V-shaped scar stood out against the flush coloring his cheeks.

Unfazed at his annoyance, she smirked and thought about what she'd do to him later. *So delicious when he's indignant,* she thought. Regardless, he wasn't the only one inconvenienced. She'd had to interrupt her day and sit in traffic to be here. The minute she hatched her plan at Forrester Research Labs, she left to pay Samuel a quick visit in the dungeon and then came directly here.

That was her definition of commitment. Some days, she wondered about his.

Usually, he embraced her midday interruptions. Not today. She didn't have time to dilly-dally anyway; she needed to take care of business.

"We're at a dead end," Em said, planting her hands securely on her hips and tapping her high-heeled Manolo. "I need more specimens, Acchie." Absent was her usual style of flirty manipulation to get what she wanted. To convey her seriousness, she had dressed the part, wearing a lab coat over her form-fitting white blouse and pencil skirt, and her dark hair was pulled back into a gleaming ponytail. The only thing that would've completed the image of her phony high-brow PhD was a pair of glasses perched on the tip of her nose. In her haste, she had accidentally left them sitting on her desk at Forrester.

Achanelech glared at her and snorted. "And how do you suppose we do that? Kidnap more Nephil babies? We don't have time to wait for them to grow up."

Sometimes he's not the brightest bulb in the box, she thought. Most days, she savored that fact.

She arched a brow. "I was thinking something more immediate . . . like snatching a Guardian or two."

He stared, speechless, as a chortle rose from his throat until laughter consumed him and tears streaked his cheeks. Clutching his stomach, he gasped for air. "Em, I do…enjoy…your sense of humor."

She felt her irises shift to black as her anger grew until it crystallized, and a snowball shot from her palm into his cackling puss.

His eyes widened in surprise as snow slid down his face. Popping out of the chair, he bubbled with ire, searing the air. "What in the name of Lucifer was that for?" he snarled as the last of the white flakes dissipated in wisps of steam from his brow.

For being such a fool, she thought. A sexy one, but still a fool. Sometimes opposites truly did attract. His fire to her ice made for an explosive relationship, in and out of bed. Although tempted to do this on her own, she begrudgingly admitted she needed his support . . . and his dungeon.

"I'll tell you, but don't take the Master's name in vain," she said, piercing him with an icy stare. "I'm not joking. I need more Nephilim. One isn't enough. We've exhausted your pet's samples.

I'm out of options. If we expect to produce this vaccine anytime soon, I need some diverse samples," she said.

He grunted and glared — the warning signal to impending obstinacy.

Changing tack to her usual approach, Em let out a deep sigh and strolled towards him, swaying her hips and wearing a sexy pout.

"Acchie, I need your help, *mon cher*," she said, pumping his ego after her little attack. His hungry gaze swept down her body, lust cracking through his look of aggravation. She sidled up behind him and sank her manicured fingers into his shoulder muscles to knead the tension that never seemed to dissipate.

"Mmm. *Cherie*, that feels magnificent, but how do you expect me to get more? With a big butterfly net? Or, better yet, we storm a Guardianship stronghold — and then what? Ask some of them to accompany us home? There's a reason why they remain elusive to us, or have you forgotten?" The more he spoke, the more his irritation sliced through his words.

Em shook her head behind him and rolled her eyes. *Why do I always have to do all the thinking?* "Do I ever come empty-handed? I have a plan, of course."

He smirked. "Why am I not surprised?"

Willing her nails into sharp points, she dug them into his shoulders.

He shook her off. Turning in a flash, he grasped her wrists. "Watch it, you're trying my patience," he warned in a low voice.

She met his hot gaze head-on. "Then don't belittle me unless you plan on finding new entertainment and procuring your own food."

He pushed away from her and paced along the Persian carpet, heat rolling off him in sizzling waves. "Must it always come down to that?" he snapped.

"No, it always comes down to something simple called *respect*," she replied, infusing a chill into her voice. Sometimes their constant bickering grated on her nerves. He'd take a couple of extra lashes for this later.

"I do respect you. Otherwise, I would've disposed of you long ago," Acchie said, waving a hand dismissively.

Bastard. As if. They needed each other too much for that. Their Master expected them to deliver on a very critical mission in the war between good and evil. An eternity of agony awaited them if they failed. Like it or not, they were stuck with each other. Given how they filled their nights, they were most definitely making the best of it. Luckily, their mutual need for control added some interesting spice to their unnatural lives.

He took a deep breath and sat down, motioning for her to take a seat on one of the guest chairs in front of his desk. He steepled his fingers. "You win, *Cherie*. I'm listening," he said. "What's your plan?"

"We hunt our prey away from the Guardianship, singling specimens from the herd. We target the Trinities," she said, wearing a wicked smile, "using your pet Nephil as bait."

Chapter 3

SAMUEL

KEYS RATTLED IN THE DUNGEON door for a second time that day, pulling Samuel out of his meditation. The door creaked open. Emanelech's twin humanoid ice minions filled the doorway…again.

"Come with us," said one of the pair.

Samuel rose to his feet and followed.

They stopped at a crude communal shower room down the hall.

"Wash." One of them shoved him through the door, and they posted themselves outside. Unlike his childhood dungeon, this one was cut into the side of a mountain. The room was constructed of solid stone, with a drain in the center of the floor and rows of shower heads along the wall.

A bar of coarse soap sat on a ledge protruding from the wall, while rags for drying himself lay in a basket at the door.

Removing the leather tie from his hair, he let it fall free and shed the filthy fabric covering his body, leaving nothing but the demonic amulet to adorn his body. He turned the knob and stood naked under the cold spray. The temperature didn't bother him, although the steam from a warm shower would've been more pleasant. At least he was alone. It had been a few years since he'd had any prison mates.

He glided the soap over the whip scars on his chest. His back bore the same lumpy crisscross patterns that started below his neck and traveled to the top of his buttocks. He soaped his hair and the places he could reach.

A sigh passed through his lips as he savored his cleanliness. He turned off the water, dried, and found fresh garments on a hook inside the door. His rags were gone.

His pulse quickened. Emanelech must've succeeded. He slipped into the loose white pants and matching tunic. After toweling his hair as much as he could with the rags provided, he secured it at the base of his neck with the leather tie and slipped on the new sandals.

Outside, his guards stood waiting. "Come."

As they ascended the stairs, the surroundings transformed from dank to luxurious. Ultra-modern artwork, expensive carpeting, and shiny objects that must've cost a demon's ransom lined the familiar hallway to the heavy yew door of Achanelech's study.

Samuel hung behind the Sphinx twins as they entered the room. Once inside, they parted, stepping to either side of the doorway and exposing him.

Achanelech stood in front of the desk beside Emanelech and leaned on his jewel-topped cane, an evil glint in his eye. Slowly, his lips twisted into a snarl, the angry V-shaped scar blazing on his cheek.

Samuel cast his gaze downward and prepared himself for a dose of the archdemon's cruelty. His shoulders stiffened before he passed through the threshold. He forced his feet to move, one in front of the other.

"Father," Samuel said softly.

With a mirthless cackle, Achanelech replied, "Mongrel, you've been promoted. Let's see if you can prove your worth as more than a lab rat. I have an assignment for you."

Samuel suppressed any outward reaction and clasped his hands tightly. "I'm at your service," he said deferentially. "Whatever it may be, I'll give my best effort."

His demonic captor looked at him with disgust and sent a burst of energy that hit the amulet resting on Samuel's chest, which instantly heated and seared the skin beneath. Samuel bit down hard as a quarter-sized welt rose and blistered under his shirt. At least it would heal, unlike the whip scars.

"Make sure you do," Achanelech said. "Otherwise, the worst torture I can think of will befall you." He glanced at the Sphinx twins. "Remove the amulet and take him to get a tracking device implanted."

A grunt emanated from one of the ice minions, and Samuel was led from the room. Relieved to be free of the demonic jewelry, he'd worry about the implications of the tracking device later. With a guarded glance, he saw a small smile play on Emanelech's lips that was meant for him.

Despite any misgivings, his spirits lifted for the first time in over a century.

PART 2: HOPE'S PRELUDE

Chapter 4

SANDRA
Haight-Ashbury, San Francisco.

SANDRA STARED OUT their bedroom window, not at the twinkling San Francisco skyline, but at the faded stars in the night sky. She felt the gentle pressure of Isa's fingertips on her upper back as he traced the invisible, nerveless scars beside her bare shoulder blades before tucking her into his chest. She shuddered against him from the chill in the room and the jarring vision that had awoken her earlier, before they'd made love. Though absent this time was the exhaustion from playing conduit for these moving picture shows.

Isa clutched her tighter. "You're worried, my beauty." His breath warmed her cheek as he spoke. It was a statement, not a question. How well he knew her. But then they'd had three hundred years — give or take — to attune to each other's thoughts and feelings. They fell just short of reading one another's minds.

"Isa . . .," she whispered his name with pained resolve. "It's almost time." The visions were intensifying and coming more frequently, leaving her to sift through a mountain of revelations for clues meant to guide her.

"I know," he said softly and kissed the top of her head.

He did know. Just not all of it, and he accepted that fact — she hoped. Her entire burden couldn't be shared without violating her oath. Instead, she discarded the bits and pieces she was sure couldn't impact his — or anyone else's — free will or destiny.

To this day, he didn't know she'd likely not survive their mission. That knowledge was hers to shoulder alone. Grateful her gift wouldn't reveal the future of those closest to her, she had no idea if he would live or die. A small but welcome mercy.

She willed her shoulders to relax and melted into his warm, naked embrace, looking for solace only he could give. His spent arousal lay nestled between them in the hollow at the small of her back, giving off a pocket of delicious heat. Her skin pebbled with gooseflesh everywhere but there, and where his smooth chest and the columns of his muscled arms surrounded her from behind.

"I'm cold," she said.

Though unable to feel normal variations in temperature himself, Isa hugged her tighter as if it would help. She'd been born Nephilim like him, but with her sacrifice to hide her origin, she had acquired human weaknesses — the heightened ability to feel cold was one of them.

She stared with longing at the sliver of December moon through the parted lace curtains. She'd never be able to feel the exhilaration of flight again, either. Her sacrifice bothered her more some nights than others. Tonight, the ache for her lost wings was particularly burdensome. Sexual release could only take her so far, while flight was wholly another pleasure. Nothing compared to soaring into the night sky with the feel of wind in her face and air coursing over her feathers. Like an amputee, sometimes she could still feel her phantom plumage.

"There must be something I can do besides hold you, my love," he said.

She turned in his arms and snuggled into the warmth of his chest. Even though she was tall at six feet, she had to look up to meet his gaze. His snow-white hair, captured in a ponytail at his nape, contrasted with his still youthful face. Eyes of the palest blue connected with hers in the darkened room. She may have sacrificed her wings and lost many of her physical abilities, but at least she retained her visual acuity in the dark.

"You're already doing it," she said and placed a soft kiss on his lips. Closing her eyes, she rested her head just above his beating heart. If the Angelorum High Council had not approved Isa to accompany her on this mission fifteen years ago, she would have refused — or at least she would've tried. His presence grounded her as she wove a life based on a false identity, waiting in a sleeper cell for the Angelorum's call.

A mission to protect the one soul whose future rode on her Trinity's success. That soul would deliver them all.

In the meantime, she waltzed in a careful dance to maintain the delicate balance between ensuring the future without breaking the rules of noninterference and trying to include Isa in whatever she could share.

"Just keep us safe, Isa. That's all I can ask." She sighed and stared up into his pained eyes. "I love you."

"I love you too, Hope," he said, using her angelic name. A name he could only use in private. To the outside world, she was Dr. Sandra Wilson. Unlike her, his name could be spoken to all. Isa, the affectionate nickname she'd given him three centuries ago. The name he'd chosen for his identity. Her lover and her mate. And, in this special case, her protective Guardian.

Her energy sagged, drawing her eyelids to half-mast. "Can we go back to bed?" she asked from inside the warm cage of his arms.

He gently tipped her chin up with a finger. "Will you tell me about the visions now? And what unsettled you so much this time?" he asked, concern etched across his white brow.

She pulled away and nodded.

They nestled beneath the covers, and she lay her head on his chest. He ran his fingertips up and down her arm in a soothing pattern. "Now, tell me."

She sighed deeply and swallowed. "I dreamt of her . . . of Cara, the First of the Holy Twelve, and of the war." Closing her eyes, she recounted the vision. "As the battle nears . . . humans . . . The Dark Ones prey on the unwilling, plucking them from the streets of the city after late-night dinners, on their way home from work, from bars, hospitals, everywhere except places of worship . . ."

"What city?"

Her heart sank. Dropping her practiced American accent, she whispered the name of their home, "*Chez-nous. Paris.*"

"Then what?" Isa asked, following her lead and slipping into French.

"They call forth demons… new ones, not yet come, who can be seen by many, not just the hunted. But it's a diversion to lure out the Angelorum…and to hide their true purpose," Hope said, describing the vision. Letting it draw her in, she connected through the Flow to the higher wisdom that lay protected within the Trinity Pool hidden inside the secret Angelorum compound.

Hope's vision shifted to the battle, and a darkened sky filled with piercing cries, blood, and feathers. "We've always assumed, somehow, that the Archangel Michael, with the support of Uriel and the Powers, would be at the center of this. But the vision paints a much different picture."

Isa's chest tensed beneath her cheek, and he whispered. "What do you see?"

Her finger traced the red Guardianship tattoo over his heart. "The battle will be led by the Twelve but will not only be fought by our fathers, but also our brothers and sisters — the Children of Uriel. Nephilim will fight Nephilim . . ."

"But how is that possible? Every living Nephilim is a servant of the Angelorum. Will there be a *Fall* among our brethren to the Dark Ones?"

She released a breath and craned her neck to meet his gaze. "I don't know yet, though I don't see anyone willingly siding with the

Dark Ones. What I do know is that Lucifer wants Cara. He needs her as much as we do. But first, something essential must happen."

"What's that?"

"We cannot let her die," replied Sandra.

Isa gave her a puzzled look in the dark. "I don't understand." She couldn't explain it all. The answers presented themselves, but she still needed time to process them. Parts of her vision were symbolic and still subject to change based on the free will and future decisions of others.

"Whatever it is that I'm destined to influence, Cara's survival depends upon it," she whispered. That was the point, wasn't it? Use her expertise for the greater good? Her temples ached from the effort of recalling the images. The next step would be to piece them together into something meaningful.

A chill settled in her bones. What she couldn't tell Isa — if her mother, Constantina, an Angelorum High Council member, and the Archangel Michael himself had not made a mistake almost six hundred years ago, the ripple in destiny threatening the First would never have happened. And she and Isa wouldn't have been implanted by the Angelorum to repair the damage . . .

Chapter 5

SANDRA
Pacific Heights, San Francisco.

"ARE YOU READY?" Isa asked her, his hand splayed on her bare back. Her evening gown hugged her curves and shimmered like light glancing over the crests of ocean waves as she walked. She'd piled her long, dark hair high on her head for the occasion, and a sapphire pendant that matched the color of her dress rested at the base of her throat. Isa strolled beside her, wearing a charcoal-gray suit to complement his pale complexion.

"As ready as I'll ever be," she replied as they headed toward the Art Nouveau ballroom in her cousin's family home for their annual New Year's Eve gala. Not truly a blood relative, Paula belonged to an old and trusted Messenger family line. As with all Messengers, if they carried the psychic gift, they loyally and clandestinely served the Angelorum.

Paula's father was one so gifted.

At the start of Sandra's assignment fifteen years ago, he had secretly secured Sandra's human identity, claiming her as a distant relative, while Paula herself remained none the wiser. Handy, given that Paula was married to the very man Sandra had been assigned to watch.

The air was thick with conversation and clinking glassware as they entered the room. Decorated in grand style, the old Victorian mansion had withstood the great quake of 1906, boasted twelve-foot ceilings, and original stained-glass windows made by Louis Comfort Tiffany.

Sandra pasted on a smile and allowed Isa to guide her in the direction of their hostess. Being the tallest person in the room, Isa had already spotted her.

"Glass of wine?" asked a server wearing a full tux as they squeezed past groups of partygoers engaged in animated discussions.

"No, thank you," Sandra said, continuing with Isa as they cut a path through the crowd toward Paula. Sandra scanned the packed room looking for Paula's husband, Dr. Tom Peyton, but found no sign of him.

Her visions had intensified earlier that day, overtaking her awakened state. She and Tom working together…racing against the clock…hiding their activities…all with the pervasive sense of being hunted. But one critical piece was still missing: the exact focus and delivery of their work.

When they reached Paula, the petite brunette threw her arms out for a hug. "Sandra! Isa! So good to see you both."

Sandra smiled and bent, taking the other woman into a warm embrace. Although both women looked to be in their late thirties, only one of them was anywhere close. Sandra had deep affection for Paula and Tom. She made a mental note that she and Isa still owed them a return dinner invitation.

"Paula," Sandra said, releasing her. "Thank you for having us."

"Nonsense, the pleasure is mine," she said, waving her hand, and then turned to Isa for a quick peck on the cheek. "Tom will be glad you've finally made it. He's been anxious to speak with you." Paula glanced around but had no more luck locating Tom than Sandra had had a few minutes earlier. With a shrug, she pulled a passing waiter to a stop. "Have a drink and chat for a few minutes?"

They all chose glasses of California red from the silver tray.

"Did you have a nice Christmas?" Sandra asked after a sip of Cabernet.

Paula gave her a disappointed smile and settled a hand on her abdomen. "It was lovely, but we were hoping for a little gift from Heaven . . . nothing yet, I'm afraid."

A heartfelt pang hit the center of Sandra's chest, and she reached for Paula's arm. "I'm sorry," she said softly. Paula had been trying to conceive for the last year but to no avail. Being Nephilim and unable to procreate, Sandra had never known maternal desire, yet she understood its importance to human women.

"There you are!" came the deep, hearty voice of Paula's father, Warner Shandwick, from behind them. A tall bear of a man with a shock of white hair, he clapped Isa on the back and leaned in to kiss Sandra on the cheek.

"Have you seen Tom?" Paula asked, wearing a puzzled frown. "I thought he might be with you."

"Ah! I think your brother has him tied up at the pool table in the game room, talking some blather involving gene pools and genetic predispositions. A load of bull hockey, if you ask me. What happened to the days when men smoked cigars and talked about the stock market, horses, and fine scotch?"

Personally, Sandra preferred the discussion on genetics.

Paula rolled her eyes and chuckled. "Not everyone can be a retired captain of industry like you, Dad."

Her father *humphed* and encircled Sandra's waist with his arm. "Be that as it may," —he glanced at Isa—"may I steal Sandra for a moment?"

Isa gave a gentlemanly tilt of his head. "Most certainly." Then his gaze connected with hers. *"If he doesn't return you within fifteen minutes, I'll follow,"* he said telepathically, using their private Trinity frequency to prevent eavesdropping in a room half-filled with telepathic Angelorum Messengers.

Warner led her through the crowded room toward his private office.

Once inside, he locked the door. The comforting smell of wood smoke wrapped around her from the smoldering embers in the fireplace. Two empty glasses with melting ice sat on the small bar, explaining the earlier fire.

"How goes it, my dear?" he asked as he pulled a flat pouch of fine leather with a round silver clasp from the top drawer of his desk and handed it to her. She suppressed a look of surprise.

"As well as can be expected," she said, replying with a mere pleasantry, unable to tell him more and knowing he wouldn't ask. Other than supplying her cover and providing the occasional message, he had no part in her mission. She ran her fingers over the smooth leather. The pouch was the signature wrapping of a privileged Angelorum communication sealed with a lock only her fingerprint could open.

"From Constantina," he added.

She smiled despite herself, eager to release the contents.

Warner headed for the door. "I'll give you some privacy. Let me know if I can be of any further assistance," he said and closed her inside.

Sandra sat in one of the leather chairs facing the desk and snapped open the silver clasp. The pouch contained only one creamy sheet of paper.

My dearest Hope,

Many blessings to both you and Isa for the New Year.

I sense your mission is almost upon you. Although this is something you must do alone, I want to express my deepest gratitude and apologize for the circumstances that have led to this necessity. We sometimes do things that we think are right, yet turn out to be wrong.

Their consequences are far-reaching, as our destinies are intricately intertwined in complex patterns of interdependency. That is the danger as well as the beauty in God's gift of free will. But you already know this . . .

Please be comforted that I will fight alongside you in this battle. I will try to undo as much as I can to set things right. But you must succeed first for me to do so.

No matter where our destinies lead us, know that I will always love and honor you. Journey forth in peace and love.

Your loving mother,
Eae

Unmoving, Sandra stared at the fine looping script, noting that Constantina had signed using her true angelic name, and ground her teeth. She folded the letter, returned it to the pouch, and stuffed it into her handbag. Rather than comforting her, Constantina's words left her with a sense of discontent and pique.

After no word for nearly a year, couldn't she have just wished them a Happy New Year and left it at that?

Now more than ever, Sandra felt like the Angelorum's sacrificial lamb. True, she had volunteered for this and had even undergone a painful and soul-crushing physical alteration to pass as human and maximize her chances of success. Yet, she couldn't help the twinge of resentment that pinched her gut. Or the blame.

She strode from the office, staring at the ground and mumbling under her breath when she crashed headlong into a passerby. They went down in a tangled jumble onto the plush Oriental rug.

Strong hands hoisted her and the man she'd fallen on from the floor in one powerful lift.

"Are you all right, my beauty?" Isa asked as the familiar brown-haired man dangling from his other hand righted himself.

Dr. Tom Peyton.

"Whoa there, Isa. Thanks for the lift, buddy. Literally." Tom brushed invisible lint off his jacket. His eyes lit up when they landed on Sandra. "Just the person I was hoping to run into — um, bad choice of words."

Sandra chuckled, returning the strap of her evening bag onto her shoulder. "Escaped the game room, I see."

He snorted. "Not before losing fifty dollars and having to defend my hypothesis about the genetic markers for longevity in the Galapagos tortoise." Tom pointed toward the noisy ballroom. "How about joining me for a drink inside? I need to check in with Paula."

"Lead the way," she said. Isa followed silently alongside her, his warm hand protectively resting on the small of her back.

Tom leaned over and whispered in her ear as they entered the room. "I'm hoping to talk a little shop if you don't mind. I could use some advice."

Déjà vu momentarily blinded her as a tingle skittered over her skin. Walking straight ahead, she nodded. "Of course."

Leaving Isa with Paula's brother to talk football and the odds of the Ravens winning the upcoming Super Bowl, Sandra stepped away with Tom. Even though she awaited her official Calling and final confirmation that Tom would be the Center Stone of her Trinity mission, she was already carefully weaving a plan. For what, she wasn't entirely sure. Sometimes her gift was as much of a handicap as a blessing. She knew both too much and not enough, often a dangerous combination.

Tom led her away from the crowd over to a frosty window beside the tall Christmas tree, brightly lit and decorated with antique glass ornaments and hand-strung garlands made of tiny gingerbread men. He shifted nervously, running his fingers through his dark locks.

"I can't talk specifics," he said quietly, his gaze surfing across the room behind her. "But I could really use your expert opinion on a few things involving a project I'm working on."

"You'll have my utmost discretion," Sandra said.

"May I stop by the University this week…and show you some samples?"

She gave him an encouraging smile. "Of course."

His shoulders lowered, the tension easing. "I'd like to learn as much as I can about your longevity and healing studies."

"I'm glad to assist in any way I can."

Excitement mixed with dread in the center of her stomach. If she were right, this was only the beginning, and her Calling wouldn't be far behind.

"Good. That's good." He shook his head and chewed on his thumbnail with an unfocused look in his eye. "I found an interesting mutation in one of my samples."

"Oh? What kind of mutation?"

"I'm not sure. Something odd on chromosome seventeen . . . but not on the test sample," Tom said, lowering his voice, "On the control sample."

Sandra raised her brows in feigned surprise and wondered what he'd stumbled upon. The possibilities were endless. "Well, between our database of study results and the Consortium we're a part of, I'm sure I can help."

If their mission involved combining their genetics expertise — she could almost guarantee it did — discovery would be the easy part. Replication. That's where it could all go wrong.

Chapter 6

SAMUEL
Menlo Park, California.

AT THE L.F. INTERNATIONAL SHIPPING COMPANY, the guard gripped his weapon and peered through the bars at the top of the heavy metal door. "Looks like he's finally out."

The technician in the white lab coat snorted. "Well, I should hope so. There was enough sedative in that dart to bring down a baby rhino."

So, this is where they're keeping them, Samuel thought. Cloaked beneath a veil of invisibility, he hung back out of the way, eyeing the row of cell doors. He'd followed the lab tech down to the prison floor on yet another reconnaissance mission to map out the inner workings of Achanelech's holdings. Cleverly hidden beneath the shipping company — the perfect cover for the archdemon's subversive activities — was a high-tech laboratory and a modern-day dungeon.

More than half the cells had to be occupied, based on the number of Nephilim Samuel had helped capture over the past year. That, and the varying tentacles of energy that tugged at him, setting his nerve endings alight the moment he'd stepped inside the dungeon — at least nine distinct signatures.

Scowling, the lab tech tapped his foot impatiently, his hands filled with syringes and a small square plastic tray that held glass vials. Keys jangled, and the cell door opened. The guard stood aside and allowed the other man to enter the darkened cell, securing the door behind him.

"How long will this take?" asked the guard through the open bars at the top.

"Ten minutes, max." The tech's voice echoed from inside.

Good. Plenty of time. Samuel wasn't due to pick up Emanelech's package at the lab for another forty minutes.

Hard to believe he was on this side of a cell door for once. Much had changed since becoming Emanelech's trusted servant. For the first time, her word had meant something.

As promised, Samuel's station had transformed overnight, giving him limited freedom and an upgraded standard of living. Released from the dungeon, he'd been moved into a small, clean room in the servants' quarters that had a real bed, modern plumbing, regular meals, and a limited wardrobe. He owned a pair of closed-toe shoes for the first time in his life. Most importantly, the random beatings and experimentation that had defined his life had ceased.

In return for his loyalty, he'd acquired a radius on his tracking device that continued growing wider. As long as he stayed within seventy-five miles of Achanelech's compound and showed up when and where he was expected, he was left in peace.

He scrubbed at his face, unnerved that his invisibility did nothing to cloak his energy from the Nephilim. He'd made that disconcerting discovery during his first capture, only then realizing why Emanelech had used him as bait.

He'd discovered that the tracker embedded between his shoulder blades had a dual purpose. Not only did the device harbor an explosive that would blow him to high Heaven if he tried escaping, but it could send a powerful and painful shock eliciting an instinctual piercing screech. A call to lure other Nephilim to come to his aid under the watchful eyes of a capturing Sphinx.

He hated his part in Emanelech's scheme, but seeing another of his kind and knowing his brethren were *real* strengthened his resolve. He no longer had suicidal thoughts. As such, Marie-Clare's message had evolved. He would do everything in his power to help these Nephilim and destroy his demon captor.

No matter the price. Marie-Clare had taught him patience to match his self-taught endurance. A powerful combination.

Like it not, he was his brethren's best hope.

Samuel ducked around a corner, out of view, and uncloaked. He'd skipped breakfast and needed to conserve energy for later. Maintaining the veil for long stretches without a hearty meal drained his reserves.

The moment he dropped the veil, the assault began. Silent, demanding voices echoed in his skull, joining the probing energy signatures.

"Who are you?" One demanded, an energy tendril tugging at his power from behind one of the cell doors.

"Identify yourself, coward!" came a second telepathic shout

His jaw locked tight. He couldn't answer.

Warriors all, there were no pleas for help among the captives. Instead, their angry voices taunted him. To them, he was nothing but a traitor, a *Rogue* who was no better than the demons imprisoning them. He understood their fury, and they had his respect. If that's what they needed to think, so be it. They had no idea his mission today would put them a step closer to freedom, or that the stars had aligned to make it possible.

If Emanelech hadn't sent the twins on another errand, the ice minions would've detected him the moment he set foot in the dungeon, though he would've welcomed their ability to block Nephilim telepathic communication.

So much for conserving energy, he thought, and cloaked to silence their voices.

Relieved to see the lab tech emerge from the cell with new samples, Samuel followed him closely up the metal stairs to the lab.

Samuel glanced over the tech's shoulder and memorized the code he punched into the keypad, adding it to his mental checklist with the code for the dungeon.

The door lock released with a soft *click.*

Only one person was inside, a dark-haired man bent over a tray with a large syringe-like object in his hand. "What took you so long?" the man asked, glancing up as the door shut behind them.

"I had to wait for the sedative to kick in." The tech grumbled, heading toward the other dark-haired man. He handed him the tray and set down the rest of his paraphernalia on the table.

"Be glad she only asked for the easy stuff this time, saliva, hair. Better than the one we have in surgery for collecting organ tissue samples. I thought he'd never go under," said the dark-haired man.

"So, how's the one in recovery?"

"Fine. The bone marrow samples are almost ready for separation," he said, still hunched over the neon green tray. "I need to doctor them up so Forrester doesn't get the whole picture if you know what I mean."

"When's the courier due to arrive?"

The man glanced at his watch. "Twenty-five minutes. But that's for a different batch." He pointed to a small box at the edge of the lab table. "Can you take their sample out of the separator and package it up?"

"Sure," the tech mumbled, and then snatched up the slender box and disappeared through a door on the back wall.

A ringtone sounded next to the dark-haired man, breaking the silence. He pressed the phone to his ear. "Dr. Romano." He scowled and bobbed his head. "Yes, that's normal . . ." His scowl deepened. "Yeah, but that's not. Give me a minute. I'll be right down."

Disconnecting the call, Dr. Romano swore under his breath and snapped off his rubber gloves.

Samuel moved closer to the lab table as the doctor headed toward the door.

A twinge hit Samuel straight in the gut, followed by a flash of heat, the warning signal his body sent before his cloak disintegrated. He dropped to a crouch behind the table where Dr. Romano had been seated and stayed put until the heavy door clicked shut. He picked up the sounds of the other man working steadily behind the rear door with no signs of stopping, and he relaxed.

Straightening, he eyed the tiny vials. The label on the tray read "Test Subject 9, bone marrow cells." He snatched three of them from the perimeter, hoping they wouldn't be missed.

He caught movement out of the corner of his eye and glanced at the reflective glass on the machine beside him. His mirror image stared back.

Damn it. His cloak had evaporated.

Grabbing another small box like the one in preparation for Forrester, he stuffed the vials inside as he strode to the door and slipped the package into a pocket inside his jacket.

Peering into the empty hallway, he stepped outside. The door shut just as the interior door opened. "Romano?"

Samuel made haste and exited using the far staircase, taking the stairs two at a time. Lucky for him, the security cameras were trained on those entering — not leaving — the downstairs compound. He couldn't cloak, but that wasn't the only tool in his arsenal. He said a prayer for swiftness, opened the door, and sped beneath the camera unseen.

Slowing to a normal pace halfway down the hall, he followed a couple of warehouse workers to the cafeteria to pick up a sandwich before he doubled back for Emanelech's package.

Samuel tapped his jacket and felt for the box, then his pocket for the cell keys he'd procured as he left the dungeon. A smile crept onto his lips. Mission accomplished.

Chapter 7

SANDRA
Stanford University. Palo Alto.

"WHEN WE ACCOUNT FOR GENE MODIFIERS—" The words froze on Sandra's tongue. She stared out at the amphitheater filled with graduate students attending her 10:00 AM Advanced Genetics class. A wisp of energy tickled the skin on her face, raising the hairs on the back of her neck.

Three weeks had passed since New Year's Eve and her conversation with Tom. He had yet to stop by and see her. In the interim, varying apocalyptic visions had plagued her dreams, turning them into a nightmarish landscape and leaving her rattled—destiny's reminder that the future was still in flux.

She counted backward from twenty. That would be all the time she had before the message from the Flow broke through on her personal vibrational hotline. If she'd been any other Soul Seeker, she wouldn't have had foreknowledge. It would've just happened.

But she was an anomaly, far from ordinary.

Finger-tapping on the one hundred-plus electronic devices in the audience ceased, expectant eyes gaping at her as the class held its collective breath.

Inconvenient was the mildest word that came to mind for the interruption. "Sorry, everyone. Please excuse me. Let's take our fifteen-minute break." Several students rose and hurried over to the podium where she stood.

Sandra turned on her heel and escaped around the corner toward the exit. Not wanting to take any chances, she stepped into a supply closet and locked the door behind her, hoping no one spotted her detour. Drawing in a deep breath, she closed her eyes and opened her thoughts to the electromagnetic stream that surrounded the earth. Like a fingerprint, the molecules of Sandra's body vibrated, connecting with her personal frequency.

"Hope, Daughter of Eae," the voice greeted her telepathically. *"It's time. The Calling awaits. You know what to do. Journey forth in peace and love."*

The wisp of power disappeared, the message complete. Had she not been filling both roles as Messenger and Soul Seeker in her Trinity, she wouldn't have had the Messenger's warning.

Her pulse accelerated. There wasn't much time before the Calling claimed her, and the soul whom she sought was revealed through the Flow. The moment that happened, her mission would officially begin, and she would be tied to that soul's essence until the mission concluded…or she died. But she already knew who the soul would be. Another anomaly unique to her implanted Trinity versus one that operated in accordance with standard principles.

She opened her eyes. Her night vision snapped on, revealing the small, cluttered interior. Open metal shelving held janitorial supplies and obsolete projection equipment, while freestanding wheeled whiteboards clogged the space in front of her.

"Isa," she called telepathically. *"It's time. I need to get someplace safe."*

His answer was immediate. *"I'll be cloaked outside your classroom. Give me two minutes."*

Reality left her with an unexpected, bittersweet feeling in her chest. After fifteen years, she'd settled into her human existence with Isa. She enjoyed their life and her research. Given her background and expertise, she still had a great deal to offer the field. Now, she prayed any legacy she created wouldn't deliver the keys to Heaven into Lucifer's greedy palm.

A loud pounding on the door startled her. "Dr. Wilson, are you in there?"

Crap. She retrieved her cell phone from a pocket in her lab coat, flipped on the light, and poked her head out the door, pretending to be on a call.

Hitting the End button, she looked up at the eager-eyed grad student and said, "Sorry, I had to take that." Turning the light off and closing the door behind her, she stepped into the hall and checked her watch.

The young woman shifted on her feet, grasping her tablet to her chest. "I'm so sorry to bother you. I really need to see you this afternoon during office hours, but the schedule says you're booked."

What is this young woman's name again?

Sandra touched the girl lightly on the shoulder and remembered. "That's okay . . . *Brenda*. That call? Personal emergency. I need to leave for the rest of the day and cancel my office hours anyway. Call Cal, he'll get you onto my calendar for tomorrow."

"I might need an extension on my experiment," she said, catching her lip between her teeth and fighting back a look of panic.

"Not to worry. We'll work it out. Would you do me a favor? Tell the class they're dismissed. Let them know I'll extend my hours tomorrow to field project questions."

Brenda nodded, relief erasing her worry, and headed back toward the chattering students.

Sandra burst through the amphitheater door into the empty hallway. A strong pair of arms gripped her shoulders, pulling her into a solid, muscular chest. She glanced down. The sleeves of Isa's campus security uniform. Fortunately, no one was around to see her disappear behind his veil of invisibility. Behind it, they could see and hear each other without anyone seeing or hearing them.

"Where shall I take you?" he asked.

Sandra rapidly scanned the hallway. "Ladies' lounge."

Isa locked the door after checking all the stalls and confirming they were alone. No more than thirty seconds later, bright light slammed down into Sandra's crown, rocking her forward on her feet. She stood frozen in place, squinting against the blinding white light. A whirlpool of energy filled her, spinning and accelerating until it radiated out of every pore in her skin, blowing Isa back a few steps.

Her Calling enveloped her, and the walls of the bathroom dropped away. Soft, harmonious voices caressed and surrounded her, lifting her spirits higher with every note. Increasing in velocity as it came down through the top of her head, the energy spun around her heart and raised her arms involuntarily from her sides.

Angelic music caressed her as a voice spoke over the melodic song, addressing her silently. *"Hope, Daughter of Eae, do you accept your place as a servant of this Trinity?"*

"Yes, I accept my place," she replied silently.

"Blessed be your journey. Hold holy your Center Stone." She shook violently as two separate strands of energy vibrated down the length of her, nearly jolting her off her feet. They intertwined and spun in a frenetic vortex, and then merged in harmony. Sandra gritted her teeth as the pressure built to unsustainable proportions, simultaneously warming and cooling the inside of her flesh. Without warning, the energy exploded outward, leaving an electric mist on the underside of her skin that prickled like a million microscopic needles. As expected, Dr. Tom Peyton's image flashed in her mind. The buzzing inside her skin was Tom—how his essence felt at the cellular level.

The music reached a melodic crescendo, and slowly the light faded. Sandra lurched to her feet, back into full consciousness.

Isa grabbed for her arm to steady her. "Now what?" he asked with a look of worry.

"Now I wait." But not for long.

Tom was on his way . . .

Chapter 8

SANDRA
Stanford University. Palo Alto.

"TOM?" Sandra stopped short inside her office door at the Wilson Longevity Lab, feigning a look of surprise at the sight of him feverishly pacing across her floor, his fingers absently combing through his mussed hair. As she expected, she hadn't had to wait long. Only twenty-four hours had passed since her Calling.

"I'm sorry to show up unannounced. I've wanted to come for weeks. I hope you don't mind, but Calvin said I should wait in here. Today . . . today . . ." He blew out a breath and pointed to the table in her office. "Let's sit. I have something to show you. I'm desperate for advice."

Sandra dipped her head and smiled serenely, wishing she could do a calming energy push like her mother. "Take a deep breath, and start from the beginning," she said, closing the door.

"It's the craziest thing," he mumbled.

Consolidating stacks of paper and journals, she cleared a space on the table for Tom to set up the laptop he clutched to his side. They huddled together so she could see his screen.

He chewed the edge of his lower lip. "I'm under nondisclosure; anything I tell you needs to stay absolutely confidential."

"I understand completely. You have both my discretion and my loyalty," she said, meeting his gaze with a focused intensity.

Nodding, he stopped chewing and keyed in his password. "I'm not sure what to make of it," he said, his gaze fixed on the screen. "About a week ago, a small package was left on the chair in my office. Whoever left it there didn't want it to be seen, but wanted me to find it. The box resembled the rest of the samples from The Foundation, the project sponsor. But it wasn't the same."

"Oh?"

Tom stopped typing. "It was addressed to a different lab. No address, just a name. JOA Labs."

Sandra frowned, unhappy to hear the news. The name meant nothing to her. She made a mental note to research them later. "A competitor?"

He shrugged. "Don't know. Never heard of them, and I couldn't find them on the web. What I think it means? Forrester isn't the only lab contracted for the work. The Foundation might be piecing the project out to multiple labs."

"Is that possible based on the contract?" Sandra asked, having almost no details about Tom's current project.

"As far as I know, Forrester has an exclusive . . ." His shoulders slumped. "I'd hoped to publish the work once we made it to the commercialization phase. That was part of my agreement." His cheeks took on a pale shade of red. "Am I being an egotistical ass worrying about that? That someone else could publish first?"

Sighing, Sandra patted his hand. "No. All research scientists dream of having their names attached to something significant." And chances were that he would. Only he'd never be able to tell anyone.

He smiled weakly. "Why don't I back up and give you some context?"

"That would help," she said, giving an encouraging nod.

"When I ran into you on New Year's Eve, I had just isolated some of the single nucleotide polymorphisms that were driving some genetic changes affecting the traits associated with longevity in some test and control mice. Then I noticed something else . . . something unusual in my earlier test subjects."

"Go on," she said, clasping her hands together.

"The telomeres that protect the ends of the chromosomes were staying intact. There was no senescence." He swallowed and locked his eyes on hers. "The mice stopped aging."

Her eyebrows popped up. "That is a breakthrough."

He shook his head. "But that's not it. That's not what I found."

A chill unexpectedly rippled down her arms, giving her gooseflesh.

Tom's eyes lit up. He pushed back his chair and rose. Suddenly animated and crackling with energy, he started pacing a rut across her floor. As his enthusiasm heightened, her skin tingled, feeling his energy through their enhanced connection. Lucky for him, it wasn't bidirectional. Lucky for her, it would make him easier to locate if that ever became a necessity.

On the downside, she'd also know if he were dead.

"The genetic material that we've been working with has never included the complete genome, only isolated genes. The package that was delivered contained samples taken directly from bone marrow from a test subject 'number nine.' I ran three samples through full genome sequencing. They had the same markers as the material we normally get, but here's what didn't make sense. The genome didn't appear on the HapMap's catalog of common genetic variants." He stopped pacing, leaned on the table, and said in a hushed tone. "Sandra? Do you know what that means?"

She stared at him, frozen. Her visions swirled in her head, her brain frantically searching for the missing pieces.

Excitement burned in his blue eyes. "The samples have male chromosomes, but whoever this guy is, there's one thing he isn't."

"What's that?" she asked, holding her breath.

"Human…he isn't one hundred percent human."

The remaining air drained from her lungs as his revelation unlocked the answer that had evaded her in the visions. The genetic legacy they would create . . . why she'd been the one chosen among all others. Clutching the edge of the table, she closed her eyes and shoved back a wave of nausea. That explained why the mice appeared to stop aging. The DNA at the base of Tom's research was Nephilim in origin. An equally disturbing thought: how had they found a donor?

Tom's fingers lightly gripped her shoulder. "Sandra? Are you all right?" Tom asked.

Opening her eyes, she nodded. "Sorry, I should've eaten breakfast. A little light-headed there for a moment. Go on."

Tom rubbed his hands together and leaned in. "I know this sounds insane, but he's *beyond* human. The only question I have is: Is this an already genetically modified human being? Or, is this how he exists in nature? Either way, what does The Foundation *really* want from me?"

Indeed. Sandra sat silently, wondering the same thing and contemplating her next move.

Tom ran his fingers back through his already tousled hair. "Say something. Tell me that you believe me."

Belief wasn't her issue. Bridging the gap between what she now knew to be the truth and how best to tell him was the problem. She laid her hand on his forearm. "I believe you . . . But maybe it's time to tell me what you're developing for Forrester."

The tightening of his brow eased. "A vaccine that can prevent disease."

"Sounds broad. Which form?"

He met her eyes. "All of them. It's meant to supercharge the immune system to eradicate every variation of disease. Even if we manage to reverse the effects of a few cancers, that's enough for me. I know. Crazy, right?"

She shrugged. "Maybe, maybe not." It would be crazy, and nearly impossible, if they weren't using Nephilim DNA. Still, something about it felt . . . *off*. Likely, there was more to the story, and quite possibly a different motivation.

"Yeah, but it still doesn't explain the halt in aging. Hey, there's one more thing." He sat back down, chewed the inside of his cheek, and pulled a slip of paper from his pants pocket.

"What's that?"

"Read it. It was in the package," he said.

She read the simple cursive and frowned at the careful letters. The handwriting looked like that of a ten-year-old child. It said, 'Trust no one here.'"

Her eyebrows flew up. *An ally? But who?* Sandra wondered. The handwriting nagged at her. "*Hmm.* Interesting." She handed the note back to Tom after stilling her trembling hand. She'd give it some thought later.

"You can do the work here. Covertly. After hours," she said, solving his most pressing need.

"Will you help?" he asked, with a hopeful gleam in his eye. "Work on this with me?"

She smiled. "Of course."

At least she had a starting point. But she held no illusions about the kind of reaction revealing the existence of angelic beings could elicit. After they survived that, all they had to do was connect the dots between Nephilim DNA and saving Cara's life. A disease-fighting vaccine? Could it be that simple?

"What did I get myself into?" he asked, dropping his head in his hands, spent.

Her stomach clenched. "Can I ask you to trust me?"

He glanced up, wearing a frown. "Of course. Why?"

She took a deep breath, wanting to ease him in slowly. "I think I know—"

A thunderous crash came from the next room, followed by a string of expletives.

Chapter 9

SANDRA

"ARE YOU ALL RIGHT?" Sandra pulled Calvin's lanky frame to his feet from underneath a jumble of fallen boxes filled with scientific journals and lab supplies.

Calvin cleared his throat and straightened his stylish black spectacles. The sheepish look on his bright red face told her that he'd been eavesdropping. He was the brightest graduate assistant she had — brilliant, in fact — despite having a streak of melodrama and a nose for getting into other people's business. In truth, she was quite fond of him.

She glanced at the vent near the ceiling and crossed her arms over her chest. "How much did you hear?"

Tom piped up next to her. "Sandra, I—"

She held up a hand to silence him, her eyes never leaving Calvin. "Answer me, Cal."

Calvin looked from Sandra to Tom, then back again, and shrugged. "Sorry, Dr. Peyton. There's an echo through the vent. I couldn't help myself after I heard that the mice had stopped aging. Longevity is the focus of my thesis."

Sandra shook her head and gave him a hard look. "That's no excuse for a lack of professional etiquette. Thesis or not, our discussion was confidential. You had no right to listen in."

He averted his eyes and wrung his hands, his neck blazing all the way down to the black Chinese characters visible on the skin above his collar. "I won't say anything. You have my word."

Maybe his nosiness was a blessing in disguise. Despite his shortcomings, Calvin was loyal, and his word was his bond. She wasn't foolish enough to think that they could do this entirely alone. *Hmm, maybe . . .*

She tapped her finger to her lips. "I have a proposal for you."

"What kind of proposal?" His eyes lit with interest.

"How would you like to work with us?"

Tom's energy spiked next to her. "But the nondisclos—"

She grasped his forearm and mumbled under her breath, "Trust me," and turned back to Calvin, adding, "But I'll need your permission."

"Permission? For what?" The subtle sounds of his respiration accelerating hit the lower range of her hearing.

"To hypnotize you. When the time is right, I'll ask, and you'll need to comply," she said.

He stared at her, puzzled. "Hypnotize me, like you did at last year's Christmas party? But why?"

"To make you forget," she said. Who knew her little party trick would pay off a dividend?

"Bu-but how will I—" Calvin stammered with a pained look of alarm.

She grasped his shoulder. "Don't worry. I'll ensure you recall the key aspects of the research that will support your thesis. But that's all. Everything else needs to go."

"Why's that even necessary?"

Sandra bit her lip, and her hand fell away. "For your safety . . . and for Dr. Peyton's. Agreed?"

Calvin shifted on his feet and nodded. "Al-l right . . ."

"We need to conceal the connection between any work we do here and Forrester. Will you help?"

"Are you kidding me? Miss the chance to find out why Dr. Peyton's mice aren't aging? I'm in." Then he broke into a wide, boyish grin and rubbed his hands together. "We talkin' corporate espionage, or what?"

Her gaze bore into him. "Closer to 'or what.'"

Tom stepped in close and whispered into her ear. "May I talk to you?"

"Excuse us for a second," she said, and they stepped out into the lab.

"Why are we involving him?"

"To do this right, we'll need help," she said. In truth, with her playing two roles in the same Trinity, she and Isa lacked a third member. To build her contingency plan, she needed another body. Choosing someone not affiliated with the Angelorum would be the most prudent course. Calvin would be better than most due to his unnaturally low threshold for hypnosis and posthypnotic suggestion.

"I don't know about this, Sandra," Tom said, locking his arms across his chest and glancing through the doorway at Calvin.

"You'll have to take this one on faith," she said, catching a glimpse of her watch. "Listen, my office hours start in five minutes."

"When do we start?" Calvin yelled from inside the storeroom.

"I'll handle Cal. Can you start tonight?" Sandra asked quietly.

He pressed his lips together and shook his head. "Paula and I…we have an appointment with the fertility specialist. It's the only time they could see us this month."

She smiled warmly. "Ah. Good luck. I know how much that means to both of you."

He blushed. "Thanks. Tomorrow night?"

"That works." She looked over his shoulder into the storeroom. "Did you hear that, Cal?"

"Loud and clear."

Suppressing a chuckle, she added *remarkable hearing* to Calvin's list of traits while returning to her office with Tom.

As Tom packed his things, his energy thrummed, hitting her in warm waves. "So, you were about to tell me something before?"

"I think it's better if I show you…tomorrow night. In the meantime, I'll ask Isa if he and his security contacts can find out more about JOA Labs and your sponsor, The Foundation." She had a sneaking suspicion of who she would find — her mother's fiery nemesis, whose territory included the North American portal to Hell just north of San Francisco.

He stopped packing, his eyes blazing with excitement. "This could be a major scientific discovery, Sandra."

"True. But one I'd bet someone else may be trying to protect. If they find out you have it…," she trailed off.

Tom's brow creased. "Do you think I'm in danger?"

Was he in danger? They all were. If not yet, then soon. She chose her words carefully, not wanting to alarm him. "Be cautious. That's all I'm saying."

AFTER THE YOUNG GRAD left her office, Sandra sagged into her chair. The afternoon had flown by in a blur of students from yesterday's Advanced Genetics class. Many were having trouble with their gene splices, or having issues scheduling time to use her lab's newest toy — a state-of-the-art, three-dimensional imaging machine with the ability to project ten-foot-high holographic images of any gene inside an intricate stand of DNA. A handy tool to determine if a splice was repaired successfully at the correct break.

The same tool she and Tom needed for their work.

Massaging her temples, Sandra contemplated a hot cup of tea to soothe her nerves while she worked through the logistics of gaining access to her lab's latest toy for herself, along with some other lab equipment on campus.

They'd need to work late at night to make this work until they could implement a permanent solution off university grounds to eliminate the risk if everything went wrong.

Retrieving a new burner phone from her purse, she dialed the Angelorum's intermediary to arrange for what they needed.

"Watson and Haskins. How may I help you?" asked a pleasant-sounding receptionist.

"Gladstone, please."

"Who may I say is calling?"

Sandra took a deep breath and then used the only name he'd know her by. "Hope, Daughter of Eae."

"Hold please." Sandra tapped her fingers on the desk, already contemplating a cover story to account for her time. The head of the department had been pushing for her to publish an upcoming project. Maybe she could use one project as a cover for the other. Still, she had to plan for every outcome.

Silas Gladstone picked up the line. "Hope? How are you, my dear?" The warmth in his voice made her smile. He and his twin brother ran the two North American branches of the firm that managed the Angelorum's private holdings — their go-to resource for anything legal or financial.

"It's good to hear your voice, Silas. I'm doing well," *For now,* she added to herself.

The niceties dispensed, Silas said, "I've been expecting your call. How can I help?"

"I have a large request, I'm afraid. I need a fully equipped genetics lab set up as soon as possible, preferably within a ten-mile radius of Stanford. I'll send a list of required equipment."

"Done. What else?"

"That's all for today," she said. There would be more later. "Let me know when the lab is ready." They said their goodbyes and hung up as Isa appeared in the doorway.

He leaned up against the jamb and smiled, his head clearing the doorway by only an inch. No longer in uniform, he was dressed in a black shirt and gray dress slacks. His hair hung loose in white waves to his shoulders, and his pale ice-blue eyes held a sparkle as he offered her a single red rose. "Happy Anniversary."

Warmed at the sight of him, she broke into a smile, but her senses ignited the moment she scented his new cologne, her gaze drawn to the ruby-red petals.

A vision gripped her from nowhere, sucking her into the Flow's vortex at lightning speed and transporting her from the room. Wind whistled past her ears and forced the air from her lungs.

A moment later, her feet slammed to the ground inside someone else's skin. Oxygen was again plentiful, comfortably expanding her chest. Her sight cleared, and a young man holding a red, foil-wrapped rose stood in the doorway.

Half a head shorter than Isa, he was a handsome blond with a lean, muscular build. His blue eyes shone, and he wore a half-smile charged with heat and desire.

Sandra's gaze darted around the room, and she swallowed, waiting to get the much-needed feed into the person she inhabited. She stood in a dorm room, and, based on her vantage point, the young woman was shorter than her by a good five inches.

He cocked a brow, pushed off the doorjamb. "You look amazing." In two strides, he was across the room, and she was in his embrace, pressed against him.

He held the rose between them. "I hope you're not allergic to chocolate. This is the closest I could come to flowers without giving you an asthma attack," he said and raised an eyebrow. "You like?"

The connection sparked, and Sandra felt her scalp tingle in response. She surrendered to the vision, taking a back seat as an observer from inside Cara Collins.

The same Cara she meant to protect.

Riding Cara's memories and emotions, Sandra stared into the man's eyes, smiled, and accepted the rose. "I like," Cara said, pretending to sniff. She was allergic to flowers, a big pain in the romance department.

Sandra caught the scent of the man's cologne…a scent both recent and familiar.

"Happy Anniversary, Car," he said, then melted his lips to hers.

Details clicked into place.

The scene was from Cara's past at Georgetown University. The man's kiss made Cara's toes curl, but who was he?

His lips were soft, full, and insistent. Her body melted into the firm muscles of his chest, while his fingers glided over her hips, pulling her closer. Cara couldn't think when he kissed her. Touching him was like some strange magic that consumed her senses.

A soft moan escaped Sandra's throat on Cara's behalf, desire setting fire to her veins. She let the chocolate rose drop gently to the rug and slid her hands down the back of his shirt, slipping them into the waistband of his jeans to rest on his warm, muscular backside. The soft, tiny hairs felt good on her palms.

Two months. That's how long they'd been dating, but it felt like she'd known him her whole life. *It should be a crime to feel this happy*, Cara thought inside Sandra's head. Since Cara had met him in September, she hadn't had one anxiety attack. Maybe things were finally changing for her.

Then again, they already had. She'd lost her virginity. Cara was glad she'd waited. The real bonus? He had just enough experience to know what he was doing. Nothing like the disastrous stories her friends had shared. If it weren't for roommates and tests, she'd happily spend every moment before Thanksgiving vacation locked inside his naked embrace. Now if she could only work up the courage to admit that she was in love with him . . .

"You sure you want to go to the basketball game?" she whispered. As much as she loved the Hoyas, she could happily skip the game in favor of more time in bed.

"*Mmm.* Maybe not," he growled into her neck and nipped her playfully. He hit a sensitive spot and she squirmed, giggling.

"Hey, that tickles," she said.

"Oh, does it? I'll show you ticklish." A teasing twinkle sparked in his eyes, and he threw her over his shoulder, tickling her with one hand while heading for her bed.

Squealing with laughter and kicking her legs, she tried protecting her midsection to no avail. "Stop!" she said, breathless.

Then Sandra understood. The important part she needed to remember. The man, Cara's boyfriend. She needed to remember his name, which came to her in a rush . . . *Kai Solomon.*

Sandra's eyes snapped open, and her muscles unclenched, giving in to fatigue.

Isa stood in front of her with the rose still in his hand. But his smile was gone. "You had a vision. Are you okay?"

She released a breath, struggling to shake off the personal violation of sharing someone else's intimate experience. Usually, she was only an observer in her visions, but on rare occasions, she would assume the identity of another person. Afterwards, it would take at least another hour to feel normal again.

"I'm fine," she lied. "I need to find a man named Kai Solomon. Whatever you do, don't let me forget his name."

"Why do you need to find him?" Isa asked.

"He's connected to Cara Collins, or at least he was eight years ago." She sniffed the air. "By the way, I think you're wearing his cologne."

Isa's brow quirked up, but he stayed silent.

Sandra clasped her hands to stop them from shaking and smiled, looking at Isa's attire and the now innocuous rose that he held. "Are we going somewhere?" Guilt clawed at her insides. How could she have forgotten the date?

His lips turned up at the edges. "That was the plan."

With a dismissive glance at the stack of work on her desk, she got up to grab her purse. Sidling close to him, she accepted the rose and gazed into his eyes. "It's still the plan . . . Happy Anniversary."

His lips descended on hers, and she welcomed their familiar warmth as he pressed her close. Her body reacted in the same way Cara had responded to Kai, though the memory of their shared intimacy unsettled her.

Isa's lips slipped from hers, and he whispered in her ear. "You forgot, didn't you?"

She squeezed her eyes shut, her cheek resting next to his, and whispered back. "A day is but a day. The one thing I'll never forget is how much I love you."

His arms tightened around her, his body shielding her in a loving embrace. Tomorrow. She'd do her part in shaping the destiny of mankind tomorrow.

Tonight would be for her and Isa.

Chapter 10

SANDRA
Haight-Ashbury, San Francisco.

WARM LIPS TOUCHED HERS, and her eyes fluttered open. "Good morning, my beauty," Isa whispered, hovering over her. "You asked me to wake you before I left."

"*Mmm.* Call me after your meeting." She stretched, trying to fight the delicious pull of the warm sheets. "And give Angel my love."

Over dinner, Isa had agreed to drive down to Los Angeles to visit their old friend and gather some intelligence. She'd be doing the same, except with her mother. Of the two of them, Isa had the far easier task.

"Meet me at the lab when you get back?" she asked, clutching her pillow.

"Of course."

Isa departed, leaving her to shake herself fully awake and review her game plan. Since her discussion with Tom yesterday, she'd been sifting through her visions, trying to fill in all the gaps.

The most important salient points were the Nephilim engaged in battle for the Dark Ones, saving Cara's life, and Kai Solomon's involvement.

Somehow, a vaccine to prevent Cara from disease or aging — while advantageous — didn't seem to be an immediate lifesaving measure. If there was one thing she was sure of, whatever they created would have to work within seconds of being needed rather than being a long-term "nice to have."

The only way to validate her hypotheses regarding Cara was to access the Trinity Stones buried deep inside the Angelorum's hidden compound. Examining Cara's Trinity Stone might yield a clue — if the stone was willing to release its secrets.

Since flying to Paris was out of the question for many reasons — not least of which was her undercover status — she'd have to use the Flow, the electromagnetic communication system that carried both healing energy and messages. To do that, she'd need access from the Irin, the Archivists who monitored and managed the Flow. But first, she'd need a High Council member to submit a request. Hence, the need for Constantina.

Though she ached to speak with her mother, that wouldn't be possible. If Constantina agreed to help, she'd be risking a lot by just placing the request, which the Council could construe as a violation of their noninterference rule. Then again, her mother owed her at least one favor. Not that she savored asking.

Sandra padded toward the kitchen, where the rich scent of brewed coffee filled the air. She grabbed her bag from the island counter and rummaged through it for her burner. If she had the luxury of time, she would've asked Warner Shandwick to pass a privileged Angelorum communication. But she didn't.

A steaming mug of caffeine in her grasp, she dialed Silas Gladstone a second time.

"Morning, Hope," he said, greeting her with his signature joviality. "What can I do for you, my dear?"

"I need to get a message to Constantina. Today."

"That shouldn't be a problem. What's your message?"

"Need access to Collins Trinity Stone ASAP. Stop. Imperative for success. Stop." She contemplated whether to add something about the Dark Ones having access to a Nephilim, then thought better of it. Chances were that her mother knew more than she did, which irked her on some days more than others. Yet, she understood and abided by the rules.

"Is that all?" Silas asked.

Knowing the weight of her request, Sandra added, "No. Add: I will not fail. Love, Hope. Stop."

She heard Silas scribbling the last of her message. "Your message will be sent immediately. I'll contact you as soon as I receive a reply."

Showered and ready to leave, Sandra's phone buzzed as she picked up her briefcase. Dropping it back to the floor, she snatched the cell from inside her purse.

"Silas?"

"No, dear one." Sandra froze, and her heart skipped a beat. She never thought she'd hear the sweet, melodic tones of her mother's voice again. "'Tis Constantina."

Fear chased away her warm surprise. "Why are you calling me directly?"

"The importance of your request warranted it," she said softly. "If I make this request for you, the other Council members will know. It's discoverable under the rules of the Twelve's Trinity Stones."

Damn it. "That's a problem, isn't it?" Sandra's hope faded.

Constantina sighed. "I'm afraid so," she said, her voice filling with sorrow and something Sandra had never heard — defeat.

To hear her mother bowing to defeat made her shudder. Constantina was one of the strongest warrior angels in the history of the Angelorum. An iron and unshakable will balanced with compassion and a fierce sense of justice, all packaged behind a deceivingly delicate demeanor.

"Why? Will it expose you?" Sandra asked.

"No. It will expose *you*," she snapped. After a long exhale, she said more calmly, "I care not for myself, Hope. But I believe there is a traitor amongst us. If I make this request, I could be placing you in even more jeopardy than you already are."

Her jaw dropped. That wasn't what she had expected to hear. Worse, there wasn't anything she could do about it. Pressing her eyes shut, she recalculated her options and potential needs. "What about you? Will this be called into question as a violation?"

"Ordinarily, it wouldn't get that far. A Messenger requesting access to another Trinity's Stone would merely be denied. But given your Trinity is an insertion connected to the Collins Trinity, I believe your request is legitimate. I'll ask Angelis, but I'm inclined to think he will agree." A close and trustworthy friend of her mother, he led the High Council.

Relieved, she vowed not to compromise her mother again.

As for her? If the stakes were higher, so be it. She already knew this mission would not end well and had accepted her fate, despite her human half's survival instinct. A weakness she despised.

She gritted her teeth. "Then do it. Put in the request. And I need one more thing. Get me access to the prophecy transcript in case I need it."

Constantina's soft breathing mingled with the silence.

"Mother?"

"I'm still here . . . Very well. It will be done," she said, her tone turning to resignation.

A pang of sorrow hit the center of her chest. "Thank you," she said softly. "I'm sorry for putting you in this position. I won't contact you again."

"I'm so very proud of you, Hope," Constantina said, an unmistakable crack in her voice. "Journey forth in peace and love, my dearest." In her life, she'd only heard her mother cry on two occasions. Both deaths. Both long ago. Once for the most recent death of her mate, and the other for the only infant she had who died.

Before Sandra could stop her tear ducts from betraying her, hot trails slipped down her cheeks. "And you," she replied, then severed the connection.

THE MESSAGE CAME, this time through the Flow, the moment after she arrived at work and sat at her desk.

"Hope, Daughter of Eae." The melodic voice greeted her telepathically. *"You have been granted access to the Collins Trinity Stone. Prepare to receive the frequency. Access will remain open for twenty-four hours. Journey forth in peace and love."*

Sandra took a deep breath, closed her eyes, and gripped the desk with both hands.

The vibration hit the top of her head first and tunneled its way down into her chest, giving her brain just enough time to memorize its vibrational pattern. Unlike her own personal molecular key to the Flow, she had to consciously recall this one. Luckily, it lodged in her mind as a distinct image, a pattern for her to visualize.

Once she knew she'd remember it, the vibrational energy disappeared, releasing her.

Excitement fluttered in her stomach as she got up to lock her office door. Maybe she'd get some answers.

Protected inside the Angelorum Sanctuary, the Trinity Pool had limited access, typically restricted to High Council members. She'd been an exception. Before she left on her mission, Constantina had taken her there to see the Trinity Stones, the eyes and ears of Heaven that held the destinies of all the Trinities. Holding as many secrets as they revealed, their life force was fueled by the free-will decisions of the souls represented within them.

Every Trinity was assigned to a tipping point that affected the final battle between good and evil. Hers and Cara's were no exception.

Sandra took her seat. Closing her eyes, she visualized the pattern that would serve as her key directly to Cara's stone. Pulled into the Flow, wind whistled past her, lifting the hair from her shoulders. Her journey lasted only seconds. The wind settled, replaced by overlapping melodic whispers in the Angelic language. A tongue she hadn't heard or spoken aloud in fifteen years.

She opened her eyes, squinting at the kaleidoscope of shimmering colors reflecting off the stone. Connected to others in a cluster, only the Collins Trinity Stone spoke while the others remained mute.

Sandra took a deep breath to get her bearings, translating the runic symbol on each point of the smooth triangular stone. A section for each Trinity member: the Messenger, Guardian, and Soul Seeker. All three sections operated separately, holding the past, present, and probable future of each soul represented. Unique as fingerprints, they pulsed at differing speeds with varying colors of light, revealing information along the stone's surface, similar to the creases on the palm of a hand. She would need the codex she had memorized as a child to translate.

Cara's stone granted only limited access, stubbornly obscuring the faces and identities of the other two Trinity members.

"What do you seek, child of Uriel?"

Jarred by the sudden intrusion of the Irin archivist, she silently blurted, *"I seek knowledge of how I might prevent Cara Collins from dying."*

"No one can be spared from physical death," the archivist answered.

Sandra realized her mistake. *"I seek knowledge on how I might help her."*

"The answer lies here. She must gain what you've lost, child."

The stone quieted, darkening except for the area containing the equivalent of the life line. A narrow, colored line shimmered along the now blackened surface in Cara's section. Then the same line in the color red lit up in the Messenger's section, followed by the purple of the Guardian's. A glow bisected Cara's lifeline not far from the point of origin, where it turned from red to purple.

The breath left Sandra as she was sucked backward into the Flow and delivered in an exhausted heap, slumped on her desk.

Sandra eased herself upright, fighting a wave of nausea. Then, the missing pieces snapped into place.

Holy Mother of God. She had her answer. Not just what this meant for Cara, but for the Dark Ones.

The Nephilim DNA wasn't intended to be used as a base for a vaccine to prevent disease or extend longevity, although both would be desirable by-products. The vaccine wasn't meant to cure Cara at all. Instead, it would be used as a delivery mechanism to transform her.

To save Cara, she must become one of the Nephilim.

Sandra had been right about at least one thing: Nephilim of the Angelorum would not *Fall*. They didn't need to. Not when the Dark Ones could genetically create their own Nephilim army.

Chapter 11

ISA
Los Angeles.

"¿QUÉ PASA, MUCHACHO?" Angel asked, wearing a broad smile as he strode across the near-empty Angel & Demons Bikers Club bar toward Isa and passed a large sign that read, "MY CLUB, MY RULES."

Rather than give an official Guardianship greeting of extended arm to shoulder, Angel clapped Isa on the back and drew him into a man hug.

Isa couldn't help but smile, happy to see his old friend.

Dark-haired and draped from head to toe in worn black leather, Angel looked his part both as owner of the bar and leader of the Avenging Angel's Bikers Club—he being "Avenging" Angel Benitez, former Guardian of the Angelorum. Almost all the bikers in Angel's club, the AABC, were "retired" Four Hundred Class Guardians who had decided to live the back half of their 400's in leisure.

At least that was the official story.

Unofficially? They were a group of Angel's contemporaries who had voluntarily followed him into exile for a crime that had stripped him of his official privileges and almost sent him to the Angelorum's version of the gallows. If it hadn't been for Constantina, that most likely would've been the outcome.

But that didn't stop some of the Guardianship leaders from calling on his services in a pinch. His intelligence connections were still second to none.

A clash of balls on the pool table behind them was followed by an eruption of Spanish curses between two patrons who ended up chest to chest, making threatening gestures with their pool sticks.

"There's a *pendejo* in every crowd," Angel muttered and gave them a sour look before ripping into his own string of rapid-fire expletives. The two men backed down, giving him a sheepish look.

Angel tipped his head toward the back. "Come on, my friend. Let's go to my office."

"*Cabrón,*" Angel called over his shoulder to one of the guys at the pool table, and nodded at a tree trunk of a man standing beside the door who made Angel's six-seven and two-fifty look small in comparison. "Behave or Hector will kick your ass back to East L A."

Angel yelled in Spanish to the bartender, an attractive young woman covered in tattoos, to bring them two Carta Blancas, then closed the door to his office.

Isa took in the wood-paneled space, which had seen better days. Paperwork covered the desk and seemed to be crawling up the walls in messy piles beside boxes of Mexican beer and name-brand alcohol stacked precariously on top of one another. Isa flicked a brow at the office's centerpiece on the back wall: a large framed photograph of a chromed-out Harley-Davidson with a busty blonde sitting astride the seat wearing immodest shorts and a bikini top.

Hope was far more beautiful, and Isa couldn't claim sainthood when it came to neatness—frequently getting the evil eye from her for leaving his undergarments in inconvenient places. Still, the office could benefit from some organization and a good cleaning. "Do you think a secretary might be in order?" Isa mused.

Angel snorted. "You kidding me? That'd be the end of my filing system." He kicked his scuffed boots onto the desk—right in the middle of a stack of invoices. "You're not here to talk about my housekeeping. What's up?"

Isa took a deep breath and clasped his hands. "What's the latest on Achanelech?"

Angel's eyes hardened. "What do you need to know?"

"Current businesses he's invested in. How he might be connected to the scientific community."

Angel frowned and withdrew his feet, dropping them to the floor with a *thud*. He leaned across the desk. "Can I ask the obvious question? Why did you drive six hours south to ask me? Why not go to Rafe?" he said, naming the Nephilim leader who ran the San Francisco Guardian House twenty minutes from his and Hope's apartment.

Isa folded his arms over his chest. "I think you know why."

A low chortle rose from Angel's throat as he laced his fingers behind his head. "This has Eae's delicate little fingerprints all over it."

Leaning forward, Isa said, "I need your discretion and your word that this goes no further. Hope's life could depend on it."

Angel stopped laughing and narrowed his eyes. "She's with you? How long have you been up north?"

Isa hesitated. "Fifteen years."

"Fif— What the hell are you playing at, bro?" Angel asked, straightening. "I thought you were fucking *visiting*."

Isa shook his head, feeling the frown etch deep into his forehead, unable to hold back the anguish he'd been carrying for the last few months. "Sorry to mislead you. We were implanted by the Council. I can't tell you much—mostly because I don't know myself. The only thing I can say is I'm afraid there's more going on than Hope can tell me." He swallowed hard over the lump in his throat. "I'm afraid I won't be able to protect her—that she'll die," he said, knowing Angel understood loss.

The type of loss that rips out your soul and leaves a gaping wound in its place—the kind of wound that never heals.

Angel's mouth pressed into a grim line, and Isa held his gaze until Angel scrubbed a hand down his face and exhaled. "Fine. I'll see what I can find out. Last I heard, he was running illegal arms."

Isa relaxed into the chair, the rigidity draining from his muscles. "Thank you."

Angel flipped his chin at him. "You working alone?"

All Isa could do was nod.

A look of concern burned in Angel's eyes. "Can I give you protection? An extra male?"

Isa shook his head. "I'll let you know."

Angel's black eyes bore into him. "Reason I'm asking is there's been talk. Incidents. It's not safe to fly solo right now."

Isa's brow furrowed. "What kind of incidents?"

Angel's jaw worked behind his cheek. "Disappearances. Nephilim falling off the grid. No bodies. Nothing."

A shiver skittered down Isa's spine, but he asked anyway. "What do you think is happening to them?"

"Dark Ones must be involved. Not sure how yet."

"Good to know." That explained the sample left for Tom. It wasn't just one Nephil like Hope thought. The Dark Ones must be capturing Nephilim to manufacture the vaccine.

Chapter 12

SANDRA
Stanford University. Palo Alto.

FINALLY, ALONE IN HER OFFICE, Sandra pulled up the Google search results on her laptop and jumped straight to the entry from *The New England Journal of Medicine.*

The gasp escaped before she could stop it.

```
Dr. Kai Solomon, a Research Scientist at
Forrester Research Labs, was presented with the
David J. Keyes Award for his outstanding
contribution to the advancement of the diagnosis,
treatment, and cure of rare cancers and blood
disorders.
```

Pressing her eyes shut, she inhaled deeply. More revelations to deal with after her earlier adventure with Cara's Trinity Stone and Isa's call about missing Nephilim.

Suddenly, the woman whose life she was meant to save was no longer at a safe distance. If Kai worked at Forrester Labs, the chances were high that Tom and Kai knew each other, which created an intersection point and vulnerability for the two Trinities.

Damn it. Not a good sign.

Methodically, she read through the rest of the entries, piecing together Kai's history and his relationship to Cara. He had grown up as an only child of a single mother who later married a plastic surgeon when Kai was in high school. Kai was now almost thirty. He'd married Melanie Jane Fishman, a retail buyer for a large clothing chain. They lived in San Jose and had a three-year-old child, Sara Solomon.

Sandra frowned, disappointed at the news after having experienced Cara's emotional bond to Kai. Then again, a lot could've transpired in the eight years since the moment she'd witnessed between them. Sadly, human mating was nothing like how it occurred amongst the Nephilim. Once she'd chosen Isa, he remained her mate for life.

Based on what she found and the small slice of Cara's memories, Sandra determined that Cara met Kai Solomon during his last year at Georgetown University, when she was a freshman. From there, he attended MIT, where he earned his PhD. Upon graduation, Kai accepted a position at Forrester Labs, while Cara remained on the East Coast, where she now resided, unmated.

Heaven, that was sad.

Next, Sandra drilled into Kai's wife's Instagram account and found a recent family photo of the three of them taken at the San Diego Zoo. They were a beautiful family. She'd give them that.

Homing in on the little girl, the child's eyes burned through the photograph and stole her breath. *What the —*

"Hey, Dr. Wilson."

Sandra inhaled sharply, her hand flying to her chest.

"Sorry, didn't mean to startle you," Calvin said, poking his head in the doorway. "Just wanted you to know that I'm back."

Her heartbeat slowed. "Thanks . . . Would you mind preparing the equipment before Dr. Peyton arrives?"

"You got it," he said, then disappeared from view.

She sighed and erased her browsing history. Starting now, she would factor Kai into her plans going forward.

TOM ARRIVED fifteen minutes later, towing a carry-on suitcase.

Sandra raised a brow. "Going somewhere?"

"Not quite," he said, lifting the case onto her newly cleared table and unzipping it. He gave her a crooked smile. "I parked at a hotel a mile from Forrester and had a cab take me back and forth to work. Told everyone I was meeting Paula at the airport and flying to Vegas for the weekend." He flipped open the top to reveal files and packaged samples. "I needed to smuggle this stuff out somehow. Ingenious, huh?"

She shook her head and chuckled. "So, what's Paula doing on a Friday night by herself?"

He laid a thick folder on the table without looking up. "She drove down to La Jolla for an impromptu spa weekend with my mother-in-law. My treat." Taking out the last of the samples, he zipped the empty suitcase and tucked it under the table.

Sandra touched his arm. "How did it go with the fertility specialist?"

His shoulders drooped, and he shook his head. "Not good. That's another reason why I suggested the trip. The last thing I wanted was to leave Paula alone with the news while we worked."

"Maybe you should've gone with her," Sandra said softly.

"With me there…," he shook his head. "No. This is better. Trust me." He picked up a folder and changed the subject. "I started to isolate some gene pairs to focus on." He eyed the big, empty platform used to display images as part of the new 3-D holographic imaging system. "Start there?"

"Sure." Deciding not to push the point on Paula, Sandra checked her watch. Isa should be back from his visit with Angel shortly.

"Here. Take a look at the first two reports while I get this set up," Tom said, thrusting out a slim folder. Then he grabbed a lab notebook and some of his samples and headed toward the imaging machine.

"Let me help you with that," Calvin said, rushing over to join him.

She sat down and opened the file to give it a cursory glance, but what they needed wasn't contained within the manila folder.

After a late afternoon phone call to Silas Gladstone, she had been granted access to the Angelorum scientific archives. The Angelorum's genetic advances were far ahead of those in the outside world, including the decoding of genomes, both human and Nephilim, as well as the associated proteins controlling gene expression.

Without that, creating what they needed would take years.

The imaging machine hummed, and Calvin dimmed the lights. Like an IMAX movie, a giant, colorful 3-D strand of DNA spun over the platform in the center of the room.

Abandoning the folder, she left her office and joined them beside the new equipment.

Tom let out a low, appreciative whistle. "That really is beautiful, isn't it?"

The doorbell buzzed. Tom and Calvin froze, and both threw her a look. "Are you expecting anyone?" Tom asked.

"Isa? Is that you?" she asked telepathically.

"Yes, my love," he replied.

"Cal, go get the door. I've asked Isa to join us."

He raced over to let Isa in. On his return, Calvin was dwarfed by Isa's hulking figure trailing behind him. The smell of Thai food wafted from the bags Isa carried, triggering a grumble in her stomach.

"Thought you might like something to eat," he said to everyone but looked directly at her. He knew her too well. She'd skipped dinner, and it was nearly ten o'clock.

"Sweet!" Calvin said, bobbing his head.

Tom smiled and touched his midriff. "Isa, my friend, you really know how to make an entrance."

A shadow of a smile crossed Isa's lips. "This is hungry work."

"Let's take the food into the lunch room," Sandra said, leading the way.

AFTER FORTIFYING HERSELF with a wide array of Thai specialties, Sandra sat back in her chair and watched Calvin devour a second heaping portion. Hard to believe someone that thin could put away so much food.

Tom dabbed his mouth, crumpled his napkin, and tossed it onto his empty plate. "Back to work?"

Sandra caught Isa's gaze, her pulse rising a notch. "In a minute. Cal, would you come with me for a second?"

Calvin set down his fork and pushed back his chair. He followed her into the hallway.

"What's up?" he asked when they were out of earshot.

She looked directly into his eyes. "Remember when I asked for your permission?"

"Bu-but we haven't even started." He scowled and ran his fingers through his hair. "I don't know anything yet."

She gave him a reassuring smile. "This is just a test, Cal. I promise."

He blew out a breath and crossed his arms. "Fine."

"Ready?" she asked.

"Yeah," he said, still sounding disgruntled.

"Drop your arms to your side and focus here," she said, pointing to the bridge of her nose. He did as he was told. To relax him, she shifted her voice to the most dulcet tones in her range. "Think about the strand of DNA in the lab, spinning around and around." She paused for a few seconds as his gaze unfocused.

"The colors are twirling and melting together . . . Lose yourself in the slow . . . spinning . . . pattern," she said softly.

Calvin's eyelids drooped, and his lips parted. He stepped back and spun in a slow circle.

Good, he's under. "Stop," Sandra said gently.

He stopped and faced her.

"You know I'd never do anything to hurt you?'

He nodded.

"Do you trust me?"

He nodded again.

"If you hear the words, 'Go to my office,' you will return to this state and go directly to my office and shut the door. You'll stay there until I come to pick you up. Do you understand?"

Dazed, he nodded, his mouth slightly ajar.

"When I snap my fingers, you'll wake feeling energetic and refreshed." Sandra counted to three and snapped her fingers. Calvin's eyes popped open wide.

"How do you feel?"

"Great! So, are you going to hypnotize me?" he asked.

Sandra suppressed a smile. "Go to my office, Cal." His shoulders and eyelids drooped. He turned on his heel and headed toward her office.

She returned to the lunch room, shutting the door behind her.

"Where's Calvin?" Tom asked, glancing over.

"I thought it would be best if the three of us spoke alone," she replied, taking a seat next to Isa and across from Tom. This was the first time they had been alone together as an official Trinity. Now came the hard part . . . telling him what it all meant.

Tom furrowed his brow and glanced at Isa. "Are we letting Isa in on the project now, too?"

She clasped her hands tightly and shook her head. "No. It's not about us letting Isa in. It's about us letting you in."

"What do you mean?" he asked, leaning back in his seat.

Giving him a tight smile, she sighed. "I think it's better if we show you. The genome you found? We know what it is."

Tom's eyes narrowed. "But . . . how . . ."

She rubbed Isa's broad shoulder and gazed into his pale blue eyes. "Ready?"

He nodded, rose from his chair, and removed his jacket. Wearing just a black Guardian T-shirt and cargos, he stepped away from the table into the center of the kitchen.

They exchanged another glance, and then slowly, Isa released his wings. The white feathers sprang from his shoulder blades and unfurled. With curving high ridges, they rose in all their lofty brilliance behind him until they touched the ceiling. He held them close to his sides since the room couldn't comfortably contain his full wingspan. For added effect, Isa unleashed the glow in his eyes and a halo of light that surrounded him when he tapped into the power of his angelic side.

He looked as if he had stepped out of a biblical drawing, just in more modern clothes.

Tom's chair fell backward as he scrambled out of it and pressed himself against the wall. Slack-jawed, he stood with his eyes riveted to Isa.

She'd expected a lot of things, but not the look of horror written across his face.

Chapter 13

SANDRA

"WHAT THE H-HELL ARE YOU?" Tom sputtered at Isa with a look of revulsion and wiped a hand down his face.

Isa dipped his head as the glow disintegrated, and his wings disappeared behind him. "I didn't mean to frighten you," he said. Her heart ached for her mate. A fierce warrior, he still had a sensitive spot when it came to prejudice and rejection—something he dealt with often due to his odd coloring—especially when it came from someone who he considered a friend.

She could kick herself for her miscalculation. Maybe a conversation would've been more effective than throwing Tom into this situation without preamble.

She walked over to Isa and gently clasped his arm. "He's Nephilim, Tom. The word is Nephilim. Part man, part angel," she said and stared up into Isa's troubled eyes. "He's been my mate for over three hundred years."

Tom slid down the wall until he was seated on the floor with his knees bent. He clutched the sides of his head. "How's that even possible? How can this be real?" he muttered.

"I'm sorry. This is a lot to take in," she said.

His head snapped up. "But you've . . . we've . . . you're Paula's cousin! How have you managed to live for three hundred years? How's that possible? Paula's known you—"

Sandra cut him off. "Paula's known me since the day her father introduced us at her college graduation party. That was the day I took on this identity. We appeared close in age, but she had no way of knowing that my aging had slowed to a crawl when I turned twenty-one in the year of our Lord 1714. As far as she knew, we were related, and Isa and I were newlyweds."

"You're not my wife's cousin?" he asked slowly, staring at her blankly. His question worried her. She tapped into their connection to determine if he was slipping into shock. He wasn't. *Good.*

Sandra shook her head. "No."

"Her father has known all along?" he asked quietly.

"Yes. Paula's family is trusted and very influential in our community."

There was no mistaking the mistrust in his eyes. "Why me? Why now?"

"Come sit," Sandra said, gesturing to the table. "I'll explain everything." Maybe not everything, but all the pieces he would need to know.

She and Isa approached the table slowly and sat down.

Tom drew himself up along the wall onto unsteady feet, dragged a chair a healthy distance away from the table, and sat.

Sandra took a deep cleansing breath and folded her hands on the table. "Samuel Clemens, a man I greatly respected, once said, *'The two most important days in your life are the day you are born and the day you find out why.'* It's the greatest truth that I've ever heard spoken."

"Wait, I've heard that before . . . Wasn't that Mark Twain?" Tom asked, giving her a wary look.

She smiled warmly. "They are one and the same. Mark Twain was his nom de plume."

"You make it sound like you knew him," he said.

She leaned closer. "But I did know him. We were both friends of Nikola Tesla. I had the pleasure of spending many days with Samuel, his wife Olivia, and their daughter, Susy, in Paris during the winter of 1894 and the spring of 1895. I was consulting with Samuel on some health issues while they were there to experience the restorative waters of the European baths. Up until fifteen years ago, that's where Isa and I lived, Paris. I've been a scientist for over two hundred years, Tom. I can spend hours regaling you with stories from my long life, but none of it matters now. What matters is what's next for all of us. Why we're all here . . . now."

Tom's Adam's apple bobbed as he swallowed. "Did he know what you were?"

She nodded. "He did. You see, he was one of our most famous Soul Seekers. His mission successfully tipped the balance toward good in his lifetime. His efforts moved us one step closer to now."

"So, is it true? Are you immortal?"

The tension in the room dropped, and she expelled a small laugh. "No, only what your test showed — long-lived. Isa will have a lifespan close to five hundred years." Her smile faltered as Isa tensed next to her. Her sacrifice had lain heavy between them for years. He would never say it, but she knew a part of him had never forgiven her for giving up her longevity for this mission. "But not me. I'll age like you now."

Tom frowned and cocked his head. "But I don't understand."

"I had to sacrifice my wings for this mission...to stay hidden from the Dark Ones. Proteins produced by glands found in the Nephilim wings control some of the gene expression in the rest of the body. One of those things is senescence . . . longevity. Removing the wings from a mature Nephilim doesn't allow the body to build alternative means to substitute for those proteins. Yet."

Not wanting to get Isa's hopes up, she hadn't told him that in the future she might have the means to restore her longevity and live out her life by his side if she survived the mission. Based on her mother's reaction earlier, her chances were probably low. But she'd worry about that later. Right now, her needs were secondary. The needs of the First of the Holy Twelve were her primary concern.

"Who are the Dark Ones?"

"Fallen angels. Lucifer and his faction of the heavenly host were cast from Heaven after the Great War. They're who we stand against."

"Knew I should've paid more attention in Sunday school," Tom mumbled. He let out a long breath and pushed back his hair with his hands. "So what is it we need to do and why?"

"We need to save a life. Possibly using the vaccine you're creating for Forrester. To do that, we need to genetically engineer a Nephilim from a human being."

He snorted. "Are you out of your mind? The field isn't even close to being ready to replicate *angels*. God…this makes no sense."

He dropped his head back into his palms.

Sandra rubbed her forehead. It would take weeks to explain everything, and they didn't have that kind of time. They had a little over a year to prepare for the day Cara would need the vaccine, but she had a strong feeling they'd get much less time than that. She had no idea under what circumstances the vaccine would save Cara. Only that, without it, they would lose the battle, and Lucifer and his minions would rule the world.

"Look at me. Do you want to be part of one of the most incredible projects mankind has ever known? With access to data the likes you've never seen before?" she asked, appealing to the scientist inside of him.

He lifted his head. "Let me guess. If we do this, no one will ever know, right?"

"I'm afraid not. But you'll know, and isn't that what matters most?"

"Can't you do this without me?" he asked.

She shook her head. "That's not how this works. Your destiny is the link to the future, not mine."

"What do you mean?" he asked.

Given the convoluted nature of their Trinity, Sandra let out a sigh and decided to stick with the basics. "Isa and I are part of a team assigned to help you fulfill your role, which is saving the life of someone very important to the Angelorum."

Tom swiped a hand over his face. "And who's the Angelorum?"

"The three hundred angel Watchers living in human form who were sent to keep the balance between good and evil; the ones who protect mankind from Lucifer and his minions. Isa and his kind, the Nephilim, are their Guardians . . . and ours."

Her words hung in the air as Tom stared at the table. Slowly, he lifted his head and looked between her and Isa, and then nodded. "Okay. I'm in. What's next?"

"We keep the Forrester project going but feed it fabricated data while we work on the real vaccine here."

"I can do that."

Isa leaned in and finally spoke. Looming over the table, he glared at Tom. "One more thing. My contacts called me on the way home. They came up empty on the lab you gave Sandra, but they traced The Foundation's funding to an offshore account of a known enemy. If these people even suspect you're onto them, they'll kill you...and your family. So don't screw up."

"And if he gets you killed, I'll kill him myself," Isa added, his words resonating telepathically in her head.

Chapter 14

SANDRA
Haight-Ashbury, San Francisco.

THE BLONDE-HAIRED CHILD stood between her parents in the observation area at the Giant Panda exhibit. She turned to see Sandra watching in her disembodied state. The child's eyes locked on hers. Blue and saucer-like, they held a sharp intelligence. Hope recognized the old soul staring back at her, and her heart skipped a beat.

Sara Solomon put her finger to her lips. "*Shh.*" When she took it away, the indentation over her top lip was gone. "Don't tell." She smiled and then turned back to look at the Pandas.

Before Sandra could react, the scene shifted, releasing her grip on the child and infusing her body with a sense of relaxation, reflecting her new surroundings.

Sandra dug her toes into the sand and leaned farther back in her beach chair, while enjoying the sea breeze off the lapping waves. Adjusting her sunglasses, she removed a book from her bag, *The Genetic Codex of Modern Mammals*, and frowned. Not exactly the light reading she'd hoped for. She dug back into her bag, looking for the romance novel she was sure she'd packed.

The sun warmed the top of her head as she poked around, not finding the book, all the while cursing herself for not wearing her new straw hat. Her forgetfulness astounded her. And where was

Isa? She suddenly noticed there wasn't a second beach chair. Why was she here alone?

She couldn't remember. The seagulls cried overhead, diving down either for fish or food left unattended on picnic blankets. What day was it, anyway?

That's right. The vaccine. They'd cracked the code. It was ready for Cara. But who had they tested it on? How did they know?

Her. They'd tested it on her. But how was that valid? She already had Nephilim DNA in her body. The sun beat down on her, growing hotter and more uncomfortable.

An uneasy feeling crept over her. Where was Isa?

She searched her bag for her phone. Sifting through all the scattered change, she came up empty. When she looked closer, it wasn't coins but shells at the bottom of her bag. Small dime- and quarter-sized seashells that sparkled in a rainbow of colors. She picked one up and caught her breath. They had the three runic markings of the Trinity Stones. Why was she holding these pieces of destiny in her beach bag?

"Dr. Sandra Wilson?" A male voice whispered next to her ear. She gasped and jumped in her seat, her head jerking around. She stared past the barrel of a gun into the sneering face of a man covered in tattoos. "Guess you aren't such a great Oracle after all," he said, and pulled the trigger. Agony ripped through her exploding skull a second before she sank into oblivion.

A scream ripped from Sandra's lungs as she sprang upright in bed. Her heart hammered as she struggled for air, trying to break free of the dream. Isa pulled her close. She collapsed, shivering next to his naked warmth.

The vision was shrouded in confusion, yet the message was clear: death would come to claim her.

"Tell me what you saw," Isa whispered, his breath heating her hair.

She clamped her mouth shut to keep her teeth from chattering. If she told him, he'd only worry. She'd spare him that, letting him believe later that Death had arrived unannounced. Isa's absence from her dream meant he wouldn't be there to save her. Another burden he didn't need to carry.

Think. She needed to think. If Death were truly on its way, she and Tom would need to tighten things up and accelerate their work. They had made excellent progress over the last month, thanks to the equipment she had managed to procure. But additional contingencies were in order. Once the last piece of the equipment arrived, they would abandon the university entirely and shift their remaining work to the hidden location.

"Hope?"

She closed her eyes and abandoned all further thought.

ISA

"ISA," she whispered into his shoulder, shuddering against him, "make love to me."

His heart pounded as he flexed his arms tightly around her, his head resting against the soft, thick hair on her crown. The sweet, familiar scent of her filled his senses. He knew every curve and crevice of her body. He'd spent his life exploring and memorizing every millimeter of it. She was as much a part of him as she was of herself, an extension of his soul.

Her fear crept under his skin, but rather than letting it hamper his desire, he used it to fuel his passion. Helplessness plagued him on many levels . . . except for this one. He lived to please her.

"With pleasure, my beauty," he whispered, and tucked her underneath him.

Her warm brown eyes connected with his as he pressed her close. His lips found hers. Soft, pliant, familiar. His body reacted to her call. He sought entrance to his version of Heaven, and with a single thrust, he found his way home.

Her shivering melted into soft, pleasure-filled moans as she whispered his name with both reverence and passion. Hands glided over the flesh of his back, sending a tingle of sensuous delight along his spine. Even after three hundred years, he never grew tired of making love to Hope. He loved feeling the press of her warm, rounded curves against him, whether in urgent need or unhurried desire. Tonight, he wanted to make it last. To savor every touch and sensation until she begged him to stop.

But he couldn't get close enough with a dark specter of dread wedged between them. Still, he tried harder, taking her to the edge of release, and then pushing her over, again and again, until they both surrendered to satisfaction and exhaustion.

Too worried to sleep, Isa lay silent and spent, cradling Hope in his arms.

"Remember the day we met? At the ceremony?" she asked softly in the darkness, twisting her finger in a lock of his hair.

"Yes...." He'd never forget. They'd met on Graduation Day for his Guardianship class during his twenty-first year. The day they'd received their red Guardianship Mark, before reporting to their assigned station. The Nephil females of the younger class had been given a box seat to witness the twenty or so males who made up the current class. Given the scarcity of females, it was only right to introduce available males to any potential mates—especially females in secular roles outside of the Guardianship. Hope had chosen to study science and nature.

The year Isa graduated, there had been only two females offered. She had been one.

When he saw her, he could barely catch his breath. Looking upon her rosy cheeks, his face had heated with a fiery blush. His coloring had drawn more than a few curious stares during his lifetime, and not necessarily in a flattering way. Rather than preening like the rest of the males, he hung back with a rigid spine and the stance of a warrior.

A smile touched his lips as he remembered. "Your lady servant came to me during the after-ceremony and expressed your wishes that I call upon you in the Meeting of the Maids."

Her fingertips gently grazed his cheek. "You were by far the most alluring male in the room."

His heart swelled, for he had believed himself unattractive as a young man with his near colorless features. Her love had sustained his life's blood all these years. She was as essential as oxygen.

He captured her hand and pressed his lips to the back of it. "I was both shocked and intrigued by your request. Never had I thought I'd be chosen over the others."

"You were always so modest," she whispered in a teasing tone as she passed her fingertip over his bottom lip. "Always underestimating your appeal."

He stroked her hair. "Perhaps it is you, my beauty, who overestimates it. Be that the case, I gladly accept your esteem."

"Were you disappointed?" she whispered.

He frowned and gazed into her upturned eyes. "Disappointed how?" The day she chose him was the best day of his life, followed by their mating ceremony.

"Disappointed that you remained stationed in France because of me. Many of the Guardians were eager to head to far-off lands in those days, where the Angelorum was needed most."

Relieved, he rested his cheek on the top of her head. "Hopefully, you will not think me unambitious, but my greatest desire has always been to live by your side."

She pressed a kiss onto his smooth chest. "Then I'm truly blessed," she said, and rested her cheek over his beating heart. "I need you to do something for me."

"Anything," he whispered and meant it.

SANDRA

NOW THAT SHE recognized Sara Solomon, she had one more person to protect—and it wouldn't be done through added security.

Reaching up, she touched the amulet Isa wore on a silver chain around his neck; the amulet that hid his energy and concealed his true nature from the Dark Ones. The request traveled over a hard lump rising in her throat. "I need you to give this to someone. Not yet, but soon."

His arms tensed around her. "Who, my love?"

"Someone who needs it more," she said softly, running her fingers over the smooth stone edges. Only twelve existed, one for each High Council member. Though the amulet Isa wore was originally meant for Hope, Constantina ended up giving it to Isa to keep him safe when Hope insisted that he accompany her. Isa didn't know that Hope had sacrificed her wings to save his—and he never would. Leading him to believe her transformation was a mission requirement, she had gone ahead before he could stop her. In truth, she feared that if he knew the amulet had been meant for her, he would've traded his wings for hers. At the very least, the Council would've demanded it.

"Then it will be done," he whispered and stroked her hair. Isa's warmth couldn't chase away the hard knot of dread that had settled in the pit of her stomach.

Now they'd both be targets.

Chapter 15

SANDRA
Palo Alto, California.

"OH MY GOD, I don't believe it!" Tom said, his voice echoing in the oversized warehouse space of their secret laboratory. His mouth hung open as he sat at the work table in the open conference area near the equipment, staring at the printed results. "Am I reading this right? The replication process gave us a one hundred percent match?"

Sandra gave him a weak smile and stayed silent. By her estimation, they were only seventy-five percent of the way there. If it hadn't been for the fact that Nephilim and humans carried so much of the same DNA, and that they had Angelorum-invented genetic replicator equipment, they'd be nowhere. So they'd managed to successfully splice the necessary Nephilim genes into a human genome and transform it into a genetically created Nephilim genome.

Now what? She wondered. Once they figured that out, all they'd have to do is bind it all up with a trigger protein that would accelerate cell replication. Then prepare a saline intramuscular delivery, and voilà. They'd have a vaccine.

Tom put down the report and reached for his unopened can of soda, eyeing her warily. "What's wrong? You should be thrilled."

He popped the top on his diet cola, took a deep swallow, and then set it down on the lab table with a *thunk.* "You're really raining on my parade. Will you tell me what's going on? You've been wearing the face of doom for a week now."

Sandra smoothed the deep furrow in her brow with a fist. "Sorry, just thinking."

He grimaced. "About what, exactly?"

Holding a hand over her mouth, she tried to harness all the problems her mind was busy trying to solve. Not least of which was their contingency plan in case of discovery.

Tom had come a long way since the night Isa revealed his true nature almost five weeks ago, diving into his new world with an open mind. So far, he'd made a formidable partner, exceeding her expectations.

"We're missing something," she mumbled, more to herself than to Tom.

He frowned. "What do you mean?"

"We're missing the 'why,'" she said.

"I thought it was to save a life."

She shook her head and paced. "That's our reason. What's theirs? It's not as obvious as creating a Nephilim army. The key to understanding anything that happens between the Angelorum and the Dark Ones is to look at the duality. It's a yin-yang relationship, a two-sided coin. Keeping Cara alive also serves Luc's purposes. and you can bet he has a damn good reason."

"Luc?" he asked, puzzled.

She flicked her hand impatiently. "Luc Morningstar is Lucifer's moniker when he's *earth-walking* in human form, or what the Dark Ones call 'living topside.' He spends the rest of his time where you'd expect."

"Of course he does." He snorted. "So what are we missing?"

She ignored his sarcasm. If he knew anything about Luc, he wouldn't be so flip. Rather, he'd have bone-chilling fear invoked at the mere mention of his name.

"Before we continue careening down the path we're on, I have to make sure we don't play right into Luc's hands. It would be just like him to manipulate us into doing his dirty work." She scratched her head and stopped pacing. "I need to spend some time digging into the Angelorum archives to study the prophecy more closely. The answer's in there somewhere."

She rose to go to the library they'd carved out of the warehouse space they were using to house their lab. Tom grasped her forearm with a look of earnestness. "Let me help."

She rubbed her lips and sighed. Two heads would be better than one at this late hour. "All right. Let's whiteboard what we know."

She rolled over the large whiteboard and erased the contents. Dividing the board in half, she labeled each side: Angelorum on the left, Dark Ones on the right.

"Let's start with the obvious. Cara needs the vaccine to transform into a Nephil to live, and the Dark Ones need it to create a Nephilim army," Sandra said, placing her notes on each side, preceded by a plus sign.

"Seems pretty straightforward," Tom said.

Sandra shook her head. "The symmetry is there, but it's too easy. We need to dig a layer deeper." She placed a negative sign on the Angelorum side and jotted down the next point. "We're breaking Angelorum Law by engineering a vaccine to create more Nephilim."

Tom's eyes widened, and he sat up straighter. "We are? I didn't know that. Why?"

She blew out a breath. "The reason Nephilim can't procreate goes back to the covenant the first Watchers broke with God during the time of Enoch. Noah, the Flood," she said, pacing in front of the board, "that all had to do with God's wrath brought down not only upon mankind, but the scourge of Nephilim abominations created by unsanctioned breeding between the angel Watchers and human women. Some modifications and new covenants were subsequently made. The Angelorum has God's blessing to be here under the protection of the new Nephilim Guardianship because of how we are created and how the Angelorum controls our numbers. This vaccine blows that all to Hell. Hopefully, not literally."

"Am I supposed to know what all that means?" he asked with a blank stare.

"For the sake of this discussion, a law has been broken. Another downside? It's a law unique to our side that doesn't create an equal liability for the Dark Ones. We can keep it at that. My only point is: why is it necessary to make Cara a Nephil to save her life?" She stopped and jotted the question underneath her negative point about breaking the law. If she had to guess, it was another by-product of the ripple she was placed here to correct. *God help me*

Tom slouched in his chair and shrugged. "I agree. Why not just harness the healing properties of the Nephilim's immune system?" He scratched his chin. "Maybe we should examine possible death scenarios. How do you think she could die?"

Sandra nodded. "Good idea." She squeezed in a third column to the left of the Angelorum column and started jotting a list: *stabbed, shot, poisoned, burned, choked…*

Tom blurted, "Car accident, explosion, head cut off —"

Sandra stopped writing and scowled at him.

"What? It could happen," he said, widening his eyes in mock innocence.

"Let's stick to possibilities that won't take a miracle to fix, shall we? Even Nephilim can't grow new heads," she muttered.

He chuckled behind her.

Her head snapped around.

"Sorry. It's late," he said, trying to wipe away his grin. "Admit it. This is kind of surreal. Isn't it?"

"Only for you," she said, and then added *illness* to the list.

"Dropped from a building," Tom said. "Kidding."

She wrote it down anyway and recapped the pen. "The sad part is any one of these things could happen, it's just that some are less likely than others."

He straightened up in his chair and took another swig of soda. "But like you said, Nephilim DNA can't help them all. Let's get rid of the least likely candidates."

She uncapped the pen and drew a line through: *head cut off, dropped from a building,* and *explosion.* "That leaves the first five, plus illness and a car accident. I think we can eliminate the last two."

Standing back, she chewed the end of the marker and stared at the list.

"Can Nephilim survive the rest of those things?" Tom asked.

"Depends," she replied, squinting at the words. "I'd lean toward yes, but so could a genetically enhanced human." She added a plus sign to the Angelorum side, followed by *accelerated healing powers.*

"This will be the first modification we need to make. Nephil heal fast, but I think we need to allow for even faster healing if any of these other five are possibilities."

Tom *humphed.* "So, then . . . what can a Nephilim survive that an enhanced human being could not?" Tom asked.

Sandra stared at the whiteboard and drew a blank.

"Okay, asked another way, what can a human *not* survive that a Nephilim could?"

"An attack by a demonic weapon," Isa said as he emerged from the hallway into the lab.

Tom thumped the heel of his hand on the side of his head. "Now why didn't I think of that?"

"Because you're only human," Isa said, fighting back a smile. Sandra was pleased that Isa and Tom's relationship had returned to normal since the reveal in the cafeteria at the Longevity Lab.

Sandra smiled, welcoming the interruption. "I guess three heads are better than two."

Isa leaned in for a quick kiss. "Possibly." He looked at the whiteboard and lifted an eyebrow. "Interesting list."

"We're trying to figure out potential death scenarios for Cara," she said. "Join us?"

Isa glanced at his watch and shook his head. "Can't. Just stopped to do a quick perimeter tour and to see if you want coffee when I come by later." He had stepped up the number of nightly patrols on the lab since last week.

Her mood brightened at the promise of hot caffeine. "That would be great."

"Affirmative," Tom said. "You're my hero, man."

Eyeing the board, Isa pointed. "Good luck with . . . that." Then he turned and disappeared down the darkened hallway.

She picked up the pen and drew lines through all the remaining options except "stabbed." "Isa's right. An attack by a demonic weapon would have a different outcome for a Nephil or anyone with angelic essence. Swords and knives are the weapons of choice for both sides. Your suggestion about getting one's head cut off is not that off base. But it would kill both a Nephil and a human, so I'd have to rule it out. But if stabbed with a demonic weapon, a human would likely not recover, where a Nephil would."

She shot him a look. "I need to take another look at the prophecy."

"But we just figured it out, didn't we?" he asked, crushing the aluminum can in his palm and tossing it into the waste bin marked RECYCLE.

"Almost. Now I have to find a way to tip the scales in our favor." Turning on her heel, she headed over to the library.

"Hey? What do you want me to do?" Tom yelled after her.

"Evaluate our options to accelerate healing. I'll be back," she paused, having no idea how long this would take, and added absently, "Eventually."

AN HOUR LATER, Tom stuck his head into the room. "Sandra?"

She looked up from her screen, bleary-eyed.

"Any progress?" he asked.

She shook her head. "The words are just melting together."

"How about a break? Isa just delivered the coffee run," he said, wearing an expectant smile and holding up two to-go cups.

Her eyes glued to the promise of caffeine in his hands, and she beckoned him inside. "Just what I needed," she said, covering an escaping yawn with the back of her hand.

He handed her one of the Styrofoam cups and then settled into a chair beside her at the library table. She took a long sip and let the warm liquid kick-start her brain.

"How'd your idea pan out?" he asked.

She swept a hand over her face and glanced at her electronic tablet. "Haven't gotten there yet. Something struck me on the way back here." She rested her stylus on the table. "The Foundation is piecing out the work to multiple labs, which both makes sense . . . and doesn't. It helps to hide their true objective, but on the other hand, knitting together a vaccine successfully with multiple teams working in silos seems a little risky. It also expands the timeline to finishing the end product. Even with the unknown collection site. Unless...." Squinting, she picked up the stylus and bit down gently on the end.

"Unless what?"

"Unless," she whispered and straightened in her chair. "Unless they already have a copy of the Nephilim Genomic Map." A shiver coursed down her spine as the pieces slowly fell into place. There was only one way the Dark Ones could have a copy of that map—a *traitor* at the highest ranks within the Angelorum. The one her mother had mentioned.

A knot formed in the pit of Sandra's stomach. Her lips parted as she followed her mind's eye back inside the beach bag to the shells and the threads of destiny that sparkled in her hand.

Cara wasn't the only one they needed to keep alive.

"What do you know about Dr. Kai Solomon?" she asked.

His eyebrows flew up. "Kai? You know Kai?"

"I know *of* him," she said, wearing a tight smile. "What can you tell me about him?"

He shrugged. "We started Forrester at the same time, and worked for a year under Dr. Lawrence Noble until his death. Kai's a brilliant scientist. Accomplished for his age."

"Anything else?"

Tom sniffed and crossed his arms. "Yeah, he's got a near photographic memory. It's uncanny. He could glance at something and spout it back to you verbatim without ever looking at it again." He chuckled. "Ironic, the guy's never on time. Was always late for meetings."

She smiled. "Different part of the brain."

"So, what has Kai got to do with any of this?" Tom asked.

"He's connected to the woman we're trying to save," she said. "They were lovers in college. If I had to guess, they're still close." She also believed, now more than ever, that Kai would play a critical role in Cara's future. There was no such thing as a coincidence in her world, only destinies to be fulfilled.

In a moment of clarity, she realized two things.

"I know how we can win this," she said. A surge of excitement lifted her heart rate. Why hadn't she thought of it sooner?

Tom's eyes lit up. "How?"

"Wings. We remove the ability to develop wings. Cara still becomes a Nephil and is saved, but the Dark Ones don't get their army."

"But I thought you said longevity . . ." he said, wrinkling his brow in befuddlement.

"Only in fully developed adults. We can separate wing and glandular development through gene modification."

She slapped the table in satisfaction, and Tom's expression turned from baffled to impressed.

Pasting on a smile, she hoped her enthusiasm would hide her second revelation . . . that neither of them would be around to see Cara live.

Chapter 16

EMANELECH
Northern California.

"WE HAVE A...*complication,*" Emanelech said, clutching her cell phone tightly in her palm as she strolled back into the bedroom she shared with Achanelech in their mansion.

Achanelech glared at her and pulled up his trousers. "What kind of complication?"

She gave him a tight smile. "According to our source, the unexpected kind."

He growled. "If you're going to ruin my day, could you at least wait until after I have a cup of coffee?"

"Fine, fine, fine," she said in a singsong voice, releasing the sash on her silk robe and pulling open her drawer of unmentionables. "Maybe I'll give Luc a call. I'm sure he'd be interested to know that the Angelorum have infiltrated our project."

"Damn it, Em!" he snapped. The bed springs creaked under his weight.

Plucking a red thong and a matching lacy bra from the drawer, she slammed it shut and faced him. He sat half-dressed in a suit, wearing an accompanying scowl.

"The early morning news delivery is what it is, Acchie. Need I remind you that it's midafternoon for our source? It could've been worse. The call could've come at three in the morning," she said. Given how they'd spent their time at three a.m., this was a far preferable option.

"What did the source say?" he grumbled, dragging a hand through his hair.

She slipped on her underwear and then pulled a suitable outfit for work from their walk-in closet.

"Well?" he snapped, tapping his clawed toes noiselessly on the Persian carpet.

"It appears my lead scientist at Forrester may be running a little side project." She shimmied into her skirt and zipped it. "His work had started to hit unexplainable dead ends at Forrester, so I had him followed."

"And?" he asked with a look of impatience.

"And," she bit out with a glare, "he's been spending time after hours in a lab at Stanford University."

Achanelech rose from the bed and shrugged. "So, how does that prove he's a threat? Besides, I thought Forrester was only assigned one portion of the vaccine development. Isn't that why we chose to use multiple laboratories? To prevent exactly that? Discovery and interference from the Angelorum? What's the connection?"

"Well . . ." She snatched a pair of gold hoops from her dressing table and threaded them through her earlobes. "I'll tell you, but you'd better not go off and do anything rash. Promise?"

He snarled and grabbed his socks from the bed. "Oh, for Lucifer's sake, just tell me." Swearing under his breath, his claws snagged the inside of the Kevlar casings as he eased his feet down to the reinforced toes. Emanelech suppressed a smile at the entertaining routine he repeated every morning. If he'd only put in the extra effort to learn an enhanced transformation spell, he wouldn't still be plagued with this problem. Demon men, a stubborn lot.

"Turns out the scientist he ran to at Stanford for help? Angelorum."

"Not exactly newsworthy, Em. You said as much already," he said, slipping on his suit jacket.

She gave him her back, a smile creeping onto her lips as she toed her way into a pair of stilettos. She'd saved the best part for last. "Would it be newsworthy for you to know that she's Eae's daughter?"

Silence. Then a low chortle rose from Achanelech's throat a moment before his arms encircled her from behind. "Sometimes you actually *do* make my day." He hissed softly into her ear, his forked tongue teasing her earlobe before he deposited a wet kiss on her neck. A pleasurable quiver traveled through her.

Turning to face him, she locked her gaze onto his coal-black eyes. She swore she could see the wheels spinning wildly behind them. Lucifer knows that, left to his own devices, he could screw up her plans. "Like I said, don't do anything rash. Our source believes they may be close to developing the entire vaccine, not just the Forrester piece. So, whatever you do—promise me you won't kill them. If they succeed, this will put us way ahead of schedule and win us favor with Luc."

"Yet. I won't kill them yet. But after they finish their work . . ." He grinned with evil glee. "Eae's offspring will make a very nice down payment on what she owes me."

Emanelech squirmed out of his grasp. "There's one thing that bothers me about this."

"What's that?"

She brushed her hair back and secured it into a high ponytail. "According to our source, she's human and not part of an assigned Trinity."

A deep frown cut across Achanelech's forehead. "That's odd. What would one of Eae's children be doing here then?"

"She left the Angelorum fifteen years ago to pursue an education in the sciences. It's not uncommon to take a sabbatical in the private sector. Coincidence, maybe?"

"Ha! Never. But you bring up a valid point. How did your source find out about this?"

"Didn't say specifically. But mentioned a second copy of the Nephilim Genomic Map was recently checked out of the Angelorum scientific archives, and that we could expect a breakthrough shortly."

Achanelech rubbed his palms together, wearing a sudden look of delight as he walked toward his cane stand with a near imperceptible limp. An affliction he blamed on Eae from a long-ago battle. The same battle where she and her mate Leo had destroyed someone very precious to him. "Ah, the poetic justice that awaits."

"Ac-chieee," Emanelech warned. "You promised. Nothing foolish, remember?"

He glared at her and puffed out his chest. "Foolish? Never. Calculated? Always."

Chapter 17

ISA
San Jose, California.

ISA STOOD CLOAKED, leaning against the Country Day School fence and scanning the children's faces until he found the one he sought. She stood alone while a group of boys kicked a ball past her, and the other children occupied themselves on a swing set and the remaining playground amusements.

Slender and tall for a child of three and one-half years, her long, silky blonde hair fell around her face as she reached down to pick up something from the ground. His gaze lasered in on her hand, where she cradled a small turtle in her palm.

"Sara, what did you find?" the young teacher asked as she approached.

Sara held out her hand. "Can we keep him?"

The teacher furrowed her brow. "*Hmm.*" Then she laid her hand on the child's shoulder and turned to one of the teacher's aides, "Crystal, Sara, and I are going to check on the old terrarium and see if we have any turtle food left."

Crystal gave them a smile and nodded.

Unfurling his wings, Isa flew in silently behind them as they entered the low-roofed building. Slipping past the door before it closed, he followed them into the classroom.

"Let me check the supply closet," the teacher said, opening a large wooden door and flipping on the light.

Standing outside the teacher's line of sight, Isa dropped his cloak.

The child stopped stroking the tiny shell with her fingertip and looked up. Her gaze filled with delight and intelligence beyond her years. "Old friend," she whispered.

A small smile crept onto Isa's lips at their mutual recognition.

Sara held his gaze and yelled, "Miss Jessica. I need to go potty."

Isa cloaked as the teacher peered around the door, holding the terrarium in her hands. "Do you want to leave your little friend in here?"

Sara smiled, walked to the teacher, and handed her the small pet. "I'll be back," she said to the teacher, then headed toward the bathroom, with Isa following. Turning on the light, she left the door ajar long enough for Isa to slip inside.

As she turned the lock, he reappeared and dropped to one knee. The child threw her arms around his neck.

"It's so good to see you, my friend," Isa said, pulling her closer.

"And you, Ishmael," she replied in a child's voice. "Living through this period of human development always makes me feel so helpless."

Isa chuckled. "An Angel Who Thwarts Demons is never helpless, no matter the form. Think of it as an unexpected advantage against your opponent."

"Rescuing turtles is my greatest strength at the moment," she said, smiling precociously. Crossing her arms over her chest, she paced and shook her head, her demeanor maturing before his eyes. "Does Eae know I'm here?"

"No. Hope sent me. She saw you in a vision." Isa pointed to the indentation over the child's lip and frowned. "I don't understand. You're *marked*." As a human angel of the Angelorum, he expected to see Sara without an indentation, or philtrum, a sign that Layela, the Night Angel, had not erased her memories of prior lives and, more importantly, of Heaven, on her soul's journey to birth.

Sara smiled wryly and touched her lip. "My father's stepfather is a plastic surgeon. He fixed my lip when I was an infant. My parents thought it was a birth defect."

A knock sounded at the door. "Sara, honey? Are you okay? Do you need any help?" her teacher asked.

"No, I'm good," she yelled through the door, the tone of her voice returning to that of a guileless child, and then her blue eyes locked on Isa. "We don't have much time. You've come for a reason?"

"Would you like me to take you to Eae?"

She gave her head a sharp shake. "Not yet. Not until after the First is Called. I must stay hidden until then."

"I understand. This will help." Isa slid the angelic amulet over his head from beneath his shirt and placed the stone on the silver chain into her tiny hand. "Hope said you must wear this."

The child gasped, her eyes widening in surprise. "This is Eae's."

Isa nodded. "Yes. She gave it to me when I accompanied Hope on this mission. To keep me safe."

Sara frowned and slipped the amulet over her head, hiding it beneath her clothes. "But what of Hope?"

Guilt seized his chest, and he averted his eyes. "She sacrificed her wings," he whispered. "I didn't know until after it was a fait accompli."

Sara's small hand touched his cheek, her expression a mask of pain. "You and Hope should never have had to pay for our sins." Throwing her arms around Isa's neck, she squeezed him into a tight hug. "I'll make this right," she said before dropping her arms.

A second knock sounded at the door.

Sara flushed the toilet. "Coming," she said, moving to leave. She stopped and looked back, her tiny hand frozen on the knob. "Journey Forth in Peace and Love, my friend. Godspeed." With that, she flung open the door and left it that way.

Isa slipped out, glancing back only once at the powerful angel trapped inside the body of a little girl who, right now, pretended to fawn over her new pet.

For the first time in over a decade, Isa had the strong desire to spend the afternoon hiding at the bottom of a bourbon bottle. A place he'd promised Hope he'd never revisit. But his longing for home suddenly consumed him, along with a sense of dread the likes of which he'd never felt before.

Even though Hope wouldn't tell him, in his heart, he knew that they might not live to see the battle they were positioning the Angelorum to win. Unlike his angelic friend, who would carry memories across every incarnation, Isa would not, nor would anyone outside the three hundred Angelorum Watchers. Isa wished he held Hope's faith in the teachings that they would be reunited in death. But in his mind, dead was dead.

"THAT'S IT," the bartender said, giving Isa a hard look. Before he could respond, his shot glass had been replaced with a steaming cup of black coffee. "It's on the house."

Isa snarled at the guy as he walked away to hide the shame swirling in his gut. Hope and Tom needed his protection, and here he was wallowing in self-pity. He glanced at his watch for the first time in hours. Even with impeccable vision, he had trouble keeping the numbers from swimming in a blurry haze. They came into focus for only a split second, but that was long enough: 6:42 p.m. He was already late.

Devil it. He'd leave the SUV in the parking lot and return to campus by air. He had pulled the six-to-two evening shift again this week, all the better to slip between campus and the new lab to check on Hope and Tom. They had stepped up their efforts over the last several weeks and were close to having a workable formula.

He pulled out his phone and swore under his breath. There were two texts from Hope sent twenty minutes ago. Lucky for him, the font was big enough to make out even as it shimmied before his eyes:

Do you have time to stop by the lab for dinner with Tom and me?

Oh, we're having Mexican. Let us know by 7 p.m.

As much as he wanted to join them, Hope would be less than pleased once she figured out how he'd spent the afternoon. He slowly punched in a reply.

Had something before work, will stop by later during patrol
Not a lie, but not the whole truth. A dull ache of loneliness gathered inside his chest. *I love you.*

Love you too, xoxo

He pocketed his phone and staggered toward the door. Halfway there, he thought better of it and took a detour to the Men's Room.

As Isa finished at the urinal and tucked himself away, a wisp of Nephilim energy curled around him and tugged. He stood up straighter and looked behind him. He was alone.

He was in Raphael's territory. His Guardians covered Northern California, many of whom Isa had met over the last fifteen years. All it took was a single meeting for one Nephil to imprint on another. But this energy footprint was unfamiliar.

Isa washed his hands and splashed some cold water on his face with his eyes glued to the mirror. The Nephil energy pulled away and disappeared.

Isa mumbled a "thank you" to the bartender on the way out, his gait having much improved with the burst of adrenaline suddenly burning its way through his bloodstream.

The unknown energy put him on alert. His muscles tensed, ready for fight or flight. He worked to shake off the remaining fuzziness in his head while something gnawed at the fringes of his memory.

He left the dark bar and squinted in the dusky light. Although steadier on his feet, driving was still out of the question. Regardless, he needed a few things from the car before he took off—his campus access badge for one.

After securing his items in closed pockets, he locked the car and headed away from the busy road to the back of the bar, where he could cloak and find adequate space for takeoff without getting hit by an incoming car.

A high-pitched Nephil distress cry sounded behind the building, followed by the wisp of power he had felt in the bathroom. His instinct to save his brethren kicked in, and he rounded the corner just as he remembered Angel's warning.

Before he could stop his momentum, his torso was immobilized in bands of fleshy steel, and the Nephil's screech ceased behind a veil of invisibility, before Isa could let out a warning cry.

An inhuman whisper echoed in his ear. "Night, night, Nephil."

He felt a sharp prick on his neck and collapsed into darkness.

Chapter 18

SANDRA
Palo Alto, California.

"DID ISA TAKE THE NIGHT OFF and forget to tell me? He never showed up for work," Miguel said. "Thought you should know in case something's up."

She pressed the cell phone to her ear and walked to the far side of the lab, leaving Tom and Calvin to work undisturbed, the sound of Green Day playing in the background. Had it been her night to choose the music and not Calvin's, Mozart would've been coming through the speakers.

"But he texted me right before seven," she said. "I thought he was already there." A quick glance at her watch showed it was ten o'clock. She wasn't expecting him for another hour or so.

"Nope. Never showed, and his cell goes straight to voicemail."

A ripple of fear passed through her. "Let me see what I can find out and call you back."

"Thanks. I'll work the rest of his shift, but he owes me one."

"Agreed," she said absently. Isa's reliability had always been his strong suit. This didn't make sense. Why wouldn't he have mentioned he wasn't at work? He'd called to fill her in after he'd dropped off the amulet before lunch, and hadn't mentioned any side trips.

She dialed his cell. As Miguel said, it went straight to voicemail. His phone was either dead or had no service. Well, she had one sure-fire way to contact him: a long-range ping on their Trinity hotline. *"Isa? Is everything all right?"*

She pocketed the cell in her lab coat and paced, waiting for him to break the silence. A sick feeling settled in her midsection after several minutes passed. Nothing trivial would keep Isa from responding. He'd given up the amulet. Something must've happened, and whatever it was, it wasn't good.

She could try one more thing, but fear constricted her lungs. No, she wouldn't do that yet. The answer might be unbearable, and she couldn't handle carrying that burden before implementing her emergency plan.

From this moment on, she'd assume they'd been found out.

She tried another call, this time with more desperation. *"Isa? Where are you? Answer me."* She stood frozen for another couple of minutes, willing an answer from the deafening void.

After texting Miguel, she strode back to where Tom and Calvin were busy at work and turned down the music.

"Team meeting. Now."

Tom's head flew up. His energy buzzed along her skin. "What's wrong?"

"Ditto that," Calvin asked with equal concern.

She pulled nervously at her braid, taking comfort in the feel of her hair beneath her fingertips, a self-soothing response she'd fallen back on since childhood. "I think the Dark Ones have Isa," she whispered through shallow breaths, not willing to think anything worse. His DNA alone gave him value. She was relieved they'd briefed Calvin a few weeks ago on the players, which would save a lengthy explanation now. It hardly mattered, since she'd erase those memories anyway.

Tom was by her side in two strides. "What do we need to do?"

Sandra took a few deep breaths and pulled herself together. She motioned for Tom and Calvin to take a seat at the team collaboration table they'd set up in an open space beside the bulk of their equipment. "Sit." She paced next to them, unable to stay still. "We have to assume the Dark Ones are on to us. We're almost there, so we can't stop now. But we need to protect the work. Hide it."

"But where? Do you think they'll find this place?" Tom asked, his gaze darting around the warehouse.

She shrugged and stroked her braid. "It can't matter. We need to keep the work in a secure location, somewhere no one would suspect. It can't stay on our person or with our effects. That would make it too easy to find."

Calvin swallowed. "What do you suggest?"

Shifting to the mental list she'd prepared a few weeks ago, she started at the top. "Cal, tomorrow, go to the post office on Cambridge near El Camino Real, rent a box under Dr. Kai Solomon's name. Pre-pay long enough into the future so we don't have to worry about the rental expiring. I'll give you a credit card that can't be tracked to us."

Tom frowned. "Kai?"

Before she answered, she turned to Calvin. "Cal?"

"*Hmm?*"

"Go to my office." Calvin's lids drooped and his mouth relaxed. Without a word, he pushed back his chair and walked away.

"What the frig was that?" Tom hissed across the table, watching Calvin plod toward the library.

She sighed. "Post-hypnotic suggestion. It's time to let Calvin go. I'll make sure he doesn't remember anything after he rents the post office box. I'll have him mail the credit card to Watson & Haskins with the keys while he's there. Then it will be only us . . . We can't endanger him any further."

Tom folded his hands and took a deep breath, his mouth flattening into a hard line. "We're not going to make it out of this, are we?"

Shaking her head, she pressed her eyes shut and told a half-truth. "I don't know. But we have to plan as if we won't." Opening her eyes, she dropped into a chair across from him. "Leave the notebook we prepared for Kai. Put it somewhere at Forrester where he'll eventually find it. Depending on how things go, it will either mean nothing to him or it will be essential for tipping him off if he replaces you."

Tom's jaw tightened. "That's a real possibility, isn't it?"

"It's possible," she said softly. "But I don't know how probable."

He nodded. "All right."

"We'll distill the research we have so far down to step-by-step replication instructions, continuing as we finish up. If this falls into Kai's hands, he may need to create the vaccine quickly. Let's help maximize his chances of success."

"Damn it, Sandra." Tom scowled and pounded a fist on the table.

"I'm sorry, Tom. Truly." Weariness washed over her. She dropped her head into her hands, wanting it all to be different. Panic bubbled up inside her over Isa. As soon as she was alone, she'd check for his energy . . . to see if it had gone dark . . . if he was dead.

Tom laid a hand on her shoulder. She hadn't heard him get up. "Let's finish this," he said, his jaw set with determination.

She took a deep breath and exhaled slowly. "Before I forget. The minute we're done, the lab disappears. Break it down if you have time. If not, there's a detonator set for five minutes behind *The Genetic Codex of Modern Mammals* in the library. Blow the place up."

His hand dropped away from her shoulder. "You're talking like I'm going to be the one who makes that decision."

She looked away, realizing her slip, and sighed. Turning back, she met his gaze. "That's a higher probability."

"I see," he said quietly.

"Promise me you won't fail," she said, fighting back the lump in her throat. She gritted her teeth. "They can't get this from us. They can't win. Understand?"

His breath hitched at the threshold of her hearing, and he nodded. "I promise."

"Let me take care of Cal. I'll be back." She hoisted herself out of the chair. Bone weary and heartsick, she headed to the library.

Calvin was seated quietly in one of the chairs with his hands folded. It only took a couple of minutes to erase what shouldn't be remembered and to implant both the short- and long-term tasks she needed him to do.

When she was done, she snapped her fingers to wake him.

He yawned. "You don't mind if I head home, do you? I'm fried."

She smiled. "No problem. I'll see you tomorrow. Wait—" Reaching behind her, she retrieved a sealed envelope from her purse. "Here. You'll need what's inside for the post office." Sandra hadn't been completely honest with Tom about her plan for Calvin from the beginning. Calvin was their fail-safe—their one remaining link. What lay locked in his head could only be released by one man . . . Dr. Kai Solomon.

"Cool."

It wasn't until Tom was gone that she noticed an envelope in his seat. Her name was written in the same childlike cursive that had been on the DNA package delivered to Tom.

Her pulse quickened. Their secret ally.

She ripped it open and slipped out the note. Her heart lurched as she read the two simple words. A sob ripped free as she clutched the paper to her chest and sank to the floor. "Thank you," she breathed.

She read it again, letting the words sink in.

He lives.

It didn't matter what happened to her as long as Isa survived.

Her relief ebbed as she looked at the note a third time and wondered when it had been delivered and, more importantly, how the messenger had gotten in and out undetected. Drying her tears, she pushed herself up and headed to the door leading into the small security closet.

She rewound the tape to the approximate time Isa called. Their only visitor was the delivery man from Rosa's, and he'd been in Tom's sight the entire time. Pressing the button on the remote, she fast-forwarded the tape to watch the delivery person enter the building.

Her breath caught. As the door was closing, it appeared to jerk slightly forward, followed by empty air before shutting. She rewound and watched in slow motion. The jerk was more pronounced this time. She fumbled with the controls and switched to the library view at the same approximate time.

He appeared from behind for only a second. A Nephil. Isa's size with blond hair gathered at his nape, dressed in black but not Guardian issue. Then he was gone, the envelope in plain view on the chair.

How odd. She'd expected their ally to be human.

Had her mother sent someone else to watch over them?

Chapter 19

SANDRA
San Francisco, California.

SANDRA GRIPPED THE STEERING WHEEL HARD, letting it bite into her palms. Anything to keep her eyes open. She wrestled to focus on the stretch of misty road illuminated by her headlights while shadowy figures of parked cars and low industrial buildings sped by in her peripheral vision.

Ten more minutes and her head could rest safely on a pillow, sadly without Isa beside her. Almost three days had passed without him . . . at least he was alive. The police had called this morning. The owners of a bar twenty miles south of San Francisco had reported Isa's SUV sitting in their parking lot unmoved for a third day in a row. That explained his cryptic text. He hadn't wanted her to know that he'd broken down and taken a drink. She berated herself for not noticing the toll this mission had taken on him and for not being there when he needed her most.

Between Isa's abduction and their accelerated schedule, she'd barely slept since his disappearance. The final vaccine was within their grasp. She was certain it would only be a matter of days before they finalized the protocol. After that, her obligation to ensure Cara's life and the future of the Angelorum would be satisfied, and then she would find her mate.

Out of nowhere, a large figure darted from the shadows in front of the car. Sandra reflexively jerked the wheel as the figure disappeared into the mist. Then, the vehicle bucked violently, yanking her hard against the seat belt. Lurching twice, the car sputtered and coasted to a stop at the side of the road.

Gritting her teeth, Sandra smacked the wheel in frustration. Why hadn't she sold the "classic" 1980s Honda to her mechanic when he'd asked? Now, she regretted not taking his offer.

She rummaged in her purse for her cell phone. It sprang to life beneath her touch, displaying the time: 1:30 AM. She located a bar within walking distance that stayed open until two. A tow truck could wait until morning. She'd summon a Lyft from the bar.

Relieved she hadn't changed into her heels from the rubber-soled lab shoes, Sandra stepped into the cool, damp night and retrieved a rain poncho from the back seat. She slipped it on, tucking her braid beneath the hood. The coat fell short on her six-foot frame, but provided enough coverage to protect her from the drizzle, which smelled of ozone and pollution.

On her way to the bar, she contemplated how to approach the final modification on the vaccine formula to ensure Cara's safety.

No more than a block from the bar, a ripple of energy sparked Sandra's senses and raised the hairs on her arms. She scanned the deserted street. The energy grew black, oppressive, and . . . familiar.

Panic rose with the realization that the shadow hadn't been a person. Dread coiled in her middle. This could only mean one thing—a Hunter demon had been sent for her.

The traitor in the High Council. She'd been found out.

Picking up her pace, a streetlight winked out as she passed, followed by another, then two more. All at once, every streetlamp flickered and exploded. Shattered glass tinkled, raining down and hitting the pavement.

Her night vision cut through the eerie darkness. Not only did she feel, but now she saw the black haze of the disembodied demon heading straight toward her. She broke into a sprint, her gaze darting between the industrial buildings, looking for an escape route.

Without Isa's angelic weapons to protect her, the demon would be unstoppable. Her only chance was to outrun it and reach a place with people before it could fully manifest.

Darting a look over her shoulder, she saw the black haze gaining on her. She screamed. The demon's energy was a hot, searing pain in her skull, ready to take her down. Strength drained from her legs as she sprinted toward a dark path between two buildings, hoping for an exit onto an adjoining street. Besides the prey warning's crushing pain, the scars on her back burned where her wings used to be.

Taking a hard left, she stumbled into an alley and grazed a building, ripping her poncho on the jagged brick exterior. Relief surged at the sight of bright lights at the end of the passageway, accompanied by the sound of late-night revelers.

Ignoring her aching lungs, she propelled her body forward.

Hooves scraping pavement signaled the demon taking physical form behind her, dashing her hopes of escape.

Death can't be cheated, she thought with bitter resignation.

The demon struck with inhuman force.

Pain radiated like a nuclear blast between her shoulder blades, lifting her from the ground and launching her twenty feet through the air. Her cheek met wet asphalt with the sickening crunch of shattered bone.

Sandra lay paralyzed with her eyes open, air whistling through her parted lips. Blood, warm and sticky, fanned out beneath her, and a severed spine dulled the scorching agony into numbness.

Demon. They had forgotten to add *demon* to the list of how Cara could die.

The demon lowered its red-skinned face to stare into her eyes, its breath heating her hair in rank puffs. Drool hung in strings from razor-sharp teeth. She knew what came next. The creature anticipated feeding before destroying her completely.

But that wasn't going to happen.

As her lifeforce ebbed, Sandra invoked the language of angels in a silent summoning prayer.

In answer, a ring of white light spread between the buildings, engulfing her and blowing her scaly nemesis off its hooves.

Embryonic warmth surrounded her, infusing her with a sense of peace. Inside the glow, a male appeared dressed in a tunic as white as the wings unfurled behind him.

His intense purple eyes gazed upon her, unlocking her memory of him. *"Jonas,"* she whispered in her mind, addressing the iconic Angel of Death.

"Old friend," he acknowledged with a head bow.

"Who's going to save him?" she asked. Without her, Dr. Tom Peyton, her research partner, would surely be next.

The angel's hypnotic purple gaze held compassion and a soothing pull. "Worry not, Hope," he said. "There are no coincidences. Only destinies to be fulfilled. The others will finish your fine work."

Expelling a final breath, she relaxed, and the silver cord severed, releasing the soul from her body. The veil of her humanity lifted, and then she understood everything, including how their work would save the one who would save them all. No longer bound to a corporeal form, she grew and expanded with indescribable joyous light.

Floating up, she glanced downward at the demon.

Enraged, it watched her ascent from below, unaware she wasn't what she'd appeared. Consuming her Nephil soul would have led to its blazing destruction.

Then, her gaze shifted and expanded outward, following the second silver cord tethering her to another. She followed it to Ishmael, where he sat, alive, in his prison cell beneath the earth's surface.

"Isa?" she whispered on the wind.

His eyes shot open in the dark. "Hope?" She couldn't be sure exactly what he saw, since she would appear in whatever form meant the most to him. Understanding spread across his face, and tears welled in his pale eyes.

"Isa, find Samuel, and protect Sara," she said.

"I don't understand," he said softly.

"You will." She sang.

"Please . . . don't go," he whispered, reaching for her.

"Take heart," she said, the pure joy of their love filling her with rapture. "I'm forever inside you, my love. We share the same soul."

She blew him a kiss that draped him in loving warmth and pulled him into a peaceful slumber. "I'll be waiting for you," she whispered in his ear and smoothed back his hair. With that, she severed the silver cord connecting them. They would reunite once he passed through Heaven's gate.

Restored to her former glory, white wings unfurled behind her. Smiling at the other angel, she offered an ethereal hand. *"Take me home, Jonas."* And together, they returned to Heaven's embracing light.

PART 3: AFTERMATH

Chapter 20

SAMUEL
Northern California.

SAMUEL TOUCHED DOWN in the Forrester Research Labs parking lot a few yards from Emanelech, where she stood arguing with a tattooed man wearing a long black leather coat and wielding a blade.

Samuel suppressed the urge to vomit when he recognized the dead man with his throat slashed at their feet. Dr. Tom Peyton's sightless eyes stared up at him, frozen in surprise. The familiar copper scent of fresh blood assaulted Samuel's senses as he watched the red pool widen around the dead scientist.

"You didn't have to kill him," she snarled at the tattooed man. "What if we still need him?"

He wiped the blade on his leather coat and gnashed his teeth. "Maybe you should've mentioned that earlier."

"Idiot," she snapped and shoved him. "Get out of my sight before I suck your soul out of your eye socket!"

Emanelech's accomplice gave Samuel a malevolent look as he passed and disappeared into the night.

Guilt settled like a massive weight inside Samuel for not predicting this outcome. He'd underestimated Emanelech. He never thought she'd make such a bold move in unprotected territory, even under the cover of darkness.

"You're late," she growled, picking up Dr. Peyton's briefcase and taking no heed of the red droplets decorating her face in a macabre pattern. "Get me out of here."

Without betraying his thoughts, he grabbed her, cloaked, and launched them both into the air with a few powerful wing beats.

A mixture of failure and fury gripped him as he flew Emanelech to Achanelech's mansion. Luckily, the rough air of high-speed flight made communication impossible. The temptation to drop her into the Pacific Ocean was powerful. Had he not feared she'd live and seek retribution he would've strongly considered it.

He had yet to discover how to kill a demon. That was his next project. Because of his ignorance, he bore the guilt of two deaths.

Two deaths he'd been set on preventing.

If only . . . He never expected Dr. Wilson's mate, Isa, to be snared in their Nephil capture scheme. The shock was overwhelming when he saw him behind the bar. Until that day, his energy had been human, just like Dr. Wilson's. He didn't understand and could only assume Isa had some power which allowed him to conceal his Nephilim essence.

Samuel knew with stunning clarity had Isa not been sitting in Achanelech's prison, he could've saved his mate.

In turn, Dr. Peyton would still be alive.

Whereas Samuel had been useless, knowing nothing of the demonic pair's plans on either occasion until it was too late.

The flaws of acting as a one-sided ally were now clearly apparent. A mistake he wouldn't repeat.

He smiled. Emanelech assumed she'd gotten ahold of the Angelorum discovery inside the briefcase. She was in for more disappointment. Tonight, would be no more fruitful than the night she had Dr. Wilson's Stanford lab ransacked.

Wrong place, wrong time, wrong information.

Samuel spotted the twinkling lights of the manse on the cliffs below. He landed at the side entrance, the one Emanelech preferred because it was closest to Achanelech's office.

He let her go, welcoming the night air to soothe the chilly burn along the inside of his arms from carrying her. The only time he felt cold was when she touched him.

"Come with me," she snapped.

He followed obediently.

She headed straight for the closed double doors. The usual trepidation crept up his spine whenever his shoes hit the Persian carpet, leading the way. "You sure you don't want me to wait outside?" he asked.

She gave him an icy glare and reached for the door. "Don't be a coward."

He cleared his throat. "Mistress?"

"Now, what?"

He pointed to the blood spatter on her cheek. "Did you want to clean that off first?"

She rubbed her face, looked at the dried blood on her palm, and shrugged. "To hell with it," she said and opened the door, clutching the briefcase.

Achanelech glanced up from his paperwork. "Whose blood are you wearing?" he asked and continued writing.

Samuel hung by the door as she sauntered over to his desk. "Rex got carried away and slashed the good doctor's throat," she said nonchalantly, and then asked with more than a little sarcasm, "Think you can muster a tad more enthusiasm for our prize?"

It was a rare day that Samuel witnessed Emanelech not in complete control of a situation. Her agitation and the quiver in her hand belied her state of mind.

Crossing his arms over his chest, Achanelech leaned back and eyed the briefcase skeptically. "Have you looked inside?"

She swung the briefcase onto the desk, where it landed with a *thunk*, and snapped the lock open. "Of course not. Who had time for that?"

He drew his eyebrows together and waved his hand at the case. "And you didn't think, perhaps, it might be a good idea to verify the contents *before* killing the scientist?"

"Of course I did! But that tattooed imbecile's idea of intimidation didn't leave much margin for error," she grumbled. "Besides, I heard him on the phone. He distinctly said that he would make the final drop-off tonight, after work. We know the Stanford lab was clean. Can it get much simpler?"

Raising an eyebrow, Achanelech said dryly. "I guess we'll find out."

Emanelech cracked open the lid, and Samuel held his breath.

Lab notebooks filled the briefcase. Achanelech's sneer turned into a genuine smile as he picked one up and opened it. Fanning through the pages, his smile faded.

"What's the matter?" she asked, picking one up and flipping the pages. "No, no, no, no!" she screamed, fanning through all the notebooks.

"They're blank. All of them," Achanelech growled. He picked up the briefcase and flung it across the room. An envelope fluttered out, addressed to "Emily."

Emanelech lunged for it and ripped it open. She ground her teeth and read it aloud. "Did you really think I was that stupid? Consider this my letter of resignation. I quit. The vaccine is safe. You'll never find it. Oh, by the way, rot in Hell, demon *bitch*." The last word came out as a high-pitched squeak. The letter spiraled to the carpet as her hands flew to cover her mouth.

Achanelech shook his head, passing a palm down his face. "Fine mess, Em. Replace him tomorrow. We'll find his vaccine or recreate it."

She stood, shaking and mewling like a wounded lamb. Ice crystals fell from her eyes onto the desk, pinging against the wood surface and bouncing to the carpet.

Achanelech rounded the desk and took her in his arms, a steamy cloud rising between them on contact. "There, there. Tomorrow is another day. All is not lost, *ma chérie*. We still have time."

Samuel looked on, shocked at the demon's tenderness. Thinking this might be a good time to leave, he backed slowly toward the door.

His movement caught Achanelech's eye. The archdemon's expression hardened. "We have one more matter to settle, Em," he said, dropping his arms. His eyes narrowed at Samuel.

"What's that?" she asked in a small voice.

"You have enough *specimens* for your experiments for now. No more."

Ice water ran down Samuel's spine as he stood rigid and motionless, rapidly assessing what this could mean for him. He needed more time.

"Bu-But—" Emanelech sputtered. Samuel hoped she'd manipulate a reasonable compromise.

"They are not pairs of shoes you can pick from shelves at the mall. Enough." An evil smirk formed on Achanelech's lips, hatred burning in his eyes. "And you can return *that* to the dungeon where it belongs. But not here. I no longer want him in my house. Put him with the others at the warehouse."

Before Samuel could react, one of the ice minions seized him from behind, the same way they'd captured all the other Nephilim.

"Acchie!" Emanelech said, throwing a regretful look at Samuel.

"Discussion closed," he snapped.

Samuel waited for Emanelech to fight back, to do *something*.

"But—but what are we going to do now?" she asked, wiping at the black smudges beneath her eyes and giving Samuel her back.

"We wait for the Angelorum's next move," Achanelech said with resignation, taking a seat behind his desk, "until we can think of something better." He pointed to Samuel. "Now, go take out the garbage."

Straightening her spine, she slowly spun to face Samuel. Devoid of emotion, she nodded to the ice minion restraining him.

"Mistress?" he whispered, dread coiling like a noose around his throat.

"*C'est la vie.*" She gave him an icy glare, shrugged, and turned to Achanelech while Samuel was dragged from the room.

Although her chilly betrayal hit with icepick precision, he'd planned for it. All was not lost.

Chapter 21

ISA
Menlo Park, California.

A WISP OF ENERGY pulled at Isa, rousing him from sleep and into the dark shadows of his cell toward the Nephilim presence he recognized from his capture.

"Who's there?" Isa growled, shaking off the disorientation from slumber, his only solace from the grief.

His sight adjusted while the fetid smell of his accommodations ripened to full bloom. A large form dressed in white prison garb came into view, sitting cross-legged in the corner of the cell. A Nephil his size but younger.

"An ally . . . and now a prisoner like you," he said quietly.

Isa frowned and snapped, "An ally? According to everyone imprisoned here, you're a traitor."

The Nephil shook his head. "No. I assisted in their capture because I had no choice," he said, his voice filled with regret.

"*Choice?* Of course, you had a choice," Isa hissed.

"Like your Hope, my choice was for the greater good. You of all people should know what that means," he accused, rising to his feet. In a softer tone, he added, "I think she'd be pleased to know that Dr. Peyton completed the vaccine."

"How do you know that?" Isa stood, clenching his hands into fists, ready for a fight if warranted.

"After you were taken, when I could get away, I tracked your mate and Dr. Peyton's progress. It was I who left Dr. Peyton the original sample."

"What do you know of my mate?"

"I know…enough," he hedged and walked from the shadows into the small area lit by the dim hall lamps shining through the bars. Blond with wary, crystal-blue eyes, he held his mouth in a grim line.

"You know she's dead?" Isa asked.

He bowed his head and nodded. "Yes. I didn't find out until afterwards. I am sorry." He looked up. "Another reason I came . . . Dr. Peyton died last night."

Pain hit the center of Isa's chest anew. Hope, and now Tom. *Lord, please help us all.*

Isa pointed at the Nephil's heart, wanting to know the lineage of the male who bore such good and bad news. "Lift your shirt and show me your Mark."

His eyebrows rose. "My what?"

Isa narrowed his eyes. "Mark. To see who birthed you."

A look of surprise crossed the other male's face. Tentatively, he lifted the hem of his shirt over his head.

Isa gasped and stepped back, his knees weakening. Missing was the red Guardian Mark he expected. In its place, deep scars crisscrossed the male's hairless torso.

"Turn," Isa whispered, an ache forming in his heart. The Nephil complied. More of the same but worse. Livid keloid welts covered every inch of his exposed skin. Indignant tears sprang to Isa's eyes. He wiped them away as quickly as they came, cursing his raw emotional state. But never had he seen a Nephil scarred such. His hatred for the Dark Ones bubbled up until bile seized the back of his throat.

"How does this give you the name of my mother?" the Nephil asked, puzzled.

Isa laid a hand on his shoulder. The male flinched as if burned by his touch, whirled to face him, and stepped back.

"Put your shirt on," Isa whispered, suppressing a look of pity. "Come and sit."

The Nephil slipped on his tunic. "Can you tell me her name?" he asked with a look of anticipation, sitting on Isa's pallet, though leaving a comfortable distance between them.

"I wish I could. This is what I sought." Isa removed his tunic, revealing the tattoo on his chest. The other male's eyes lit up.

Isa pointed to the crest at the bottom. "This symbol," he said, "represents the Angelorum Guardianship. Right here, above it, is my name written in the angelic language. It says, 'Ishmael, Son of Derdekea.' Derdekea is my mother."

The Nephil's expression crumbled into a look of disappointment. Hanging his head, he pulled a piece of straw from the mattress. "So, you can't tell me who my mother is," he said flatly.

"Tell me who you are," Isa coaxed. "Even without a Mark, I may be able to help."

He released a breath. "As far back as I can remember, the archdemon called Achanelech has claimed he's my father and that my mother abandoned me, leaving me in his clutches. I was punished for merely drawing breath . . ."

Isa listened patiently as the male told him of Marie-Claire and her prophesy, his years of solitude and neglect, the lifeline given to him by Achanelech's consort, how Isa's capture had been a mistake, and what he'd gleaned so far on the inner workings of Achanelech's holdings—including how he came to have a key to Isa's cell.

One thing was certain. Isa believed him and had found an ally. By the time the Collins Trinity arrived, they would be ready.

After the male finished, Isa sat back and smiled. "Do you realize that you've still not told me your name?"

The side of the Nephil's mouth quirked up in a half-smile. "Maybe it's because no one has ever cared to ask. Samuel . . . my name is Samuel."

Isa's chest filled with warmth, and his eyes welled as he remembered Hope's parting words, *"Find Samuel."* He didn't have to. Samuel had found him. Isa took a deep breath and swallowed. "Extend your arm and place it on my shoulder."

Samuel hesitated and then did as he was told.

"May I do the same?" Isa asked, sensing the other male's discomfort with physical contact.

Pressing his lips together, Samuel nodded.

Isa rested his hand on Samuel and said telepathically. *"This is an official Guardianship greeting. From this day forward, I call you* brother."

Samuel's jaw locked, and he turned away. But not before Isa saw his glistening tears.

"I think I know who birthed you," Isa whispered.

Samuel's head jerked back, his wet eyes eager.

"She will come for us," Isa said.

"How do you know?" Samuel asked.

Isa squeezed Samuel's shoulder and gave him a reassuring smile. "Because she is an Angel Who Thwarts Demons."

Thus, the Story Begins…

Want more Angelorum Twelve?

Dear Reader,

Thank you for entering the World of the Angelorum! I hope you enjoyed HOPE'S PRELUDE.

The Angelorum Twelve Chronicles is an epic story told across four books, plus this prequel novella (Book 2.5), which divides the series and reveals secrets and introduces characters (living and dead) from the first two books, starting with a prologue in TRINITY STONES (Book 1). Samuel's journey, Sandra & Tom's heroic sacrifice, and Sandra & Isa's love story, are integral to the Twelve, and they all deserve their part in this story.

If this is your first trip into the world of the Angelorum, I hope you'll try the series from the beginning and fall in love with the characters as much as I did. Each book — including this one — can be read to a satisfying conclusion.

Previews of all the published & preorder books in the series, starting with TRINITY STONES (Book 1), can be found on my website's download page: https://lgoconnor.com/downloads/

Although this novella isn't steamy, the novels average 3.5 on a scale of 1-5.

Consider leaving a review on Amazon, Goodreads, or sharing on Instagram or TikTok (#BookTok). Please and thank you! Truly, word of mouth is what helps authors sell books.

Hugs & Happy Reading!

L.G.

The Angelorum Twelve Books & Reading Order

*From L.G. O'Connor, award-winning author of **Caught Up in Raine**, comes a 4-book epic angel & demon fantasy series with forbidden and fated love, enemies-to-lovers, found family, and sizzling romance that will leave you wanting more.*

Science and spirit meet in The Angelorum Twelve, an epic angel & demon fantasy. For 2,000 years, the Angelorum — the next generation of angelic Watchers — has maintained the balance of good and evil between humanity and Lucifer's Dark Ones. Both sides have played by the rules...until now. Lucifer has a score to settle and a celestial loophole to seize to restore his rightful place in the final battle of good and evil. Twelve souls will stretch the limits of Heaven and Earth to stop him...

TRINITY STONES, Book One.

There are no coincidences, only destinies to be fulfilled.

Cara Collins is questioning her choices. Between a back-stabbing boss, a non-existent social life, and lingering feelings for Dr. Kai Solomon, a man she can never have, things need to change. After discovering she has the power to restore the gift of youth the same day she receives an unexpected $50 million windfall, it seems Fate agrees.

Learning she is part of a Trinity, Cara is shaken to discover she can become the angelic weapon needed to defeat Lucifer and his Dark Ones in their quest to conquer Heaven and enslave humanity. Torn between her duty to save the world and the promise of a new love, the timing couldn't be worse.

Cara's unseen Nephilim Guardian, Chamuel, knows he has a problem the moment he sees his new charge. His heart stirs for the first time in over a century for the one female on earth forbidden to him under Angelorum Law. After a chance encounter under his human identity, he's powerless to resist her—regardless of the devastating price he will pay if anyone, including Cara, discovers the truth.

When dark forces kidnap Kai and his daughter, forbidden love, betrayal, and destiny collide, forcing Cara to make an impossible choice to save the people she loves without sacrificing the future of humanity, and playing right into Lucifer's hands.

WANDERER'S CHILDREN, Book Two.

Los Angeles. San Francisco. Chicago. New York. The Wanderer's mission three decades ago: secretly sire children to hide his bloodline, and protect them until their destinies unite to fight the final battle between good and evil.

Duty will call soon to gather the rest of the Angelorum Twelve and prepare them for battle. Before that happens, Cara Collins wants one peaceful weekend with her bridesmaids before her wedding to her former Trinity Guardian. But we don't always get what we want …

Life has changed. Cara's newly acquired Nephilim DNA is wreaking havoc on her body, with an overabundance of pheromones triggering a mortifying outbreak of "insta-love" among her friends that would make Cupid proud. If only she could point her arrow at her Trinity Messenger, Michael Swift, who has been running from his attraction to Cara's brazen best friend, Sienna, the only woman ever to skirt his defenses. Even if he wants a future with her, first, he must confront his tormented past, or risk threatening the future of the Angelorum.

After a chance encounter, runaway rock star Brett King is harboring a crush on Cara, but, infatuation aside, Brett is more than he appears. One of the Wanderer's children he and his siblings are the key to gathering the rest of the Twelve souls destined to fight in the final battle of good and evil. With the growing threat of Lucifer's fallen angels, Cara has more to worry about than petty jealousy, drunken debauchery, and a bridal shower. An enemy within the Angelorum is determined to see them fail, if a traitor in Cara's inner circle doesn't destroy them all.

HOPE'S PRELUDE, Prequel Novella, Book 2.5.

Save the *One* who will save them all.

Enter the world of the Angelorum for a glimpse into its origins as destinies entwine to deliver us one step closer to battle …

Stolen as an infant by Achanelech, the Archdemon of Fire, Samuel has lived in his kidnapper's dungeons for over a century. Unaware of his angelic origins, he is persuaded to help capture his Nephilim brethren in exchange for a longer leash and a chance to plot his own escape.

While dealing with visions of her death, Dr. Sandra Wilson races against the clock with research partner, Dr. Tom Peyton and her Nephilim mate, Isa, to develop a vaccine that will save the One.

With Isa ensnared in Achanelech's trap, and the Archdemon closing in on Sandra, it is Samuel who must risk his freedom to ensure the future of the Angelorum … and the mother he never met.

About the Author

Photo: Oak & Ivy Photograph

L.G. O'Connor spends her free time spinning fantasy, contemporary, and mystery stories that touch the heart with themes of family, redemption, forgiveness, and above all, hope. An avid reader, she loves books with memorable characters that linger long after the story ends.

L.G. is the author of the multi-award-winning romantic women's fiction trilogy: *Caught Up in Raine, Shelter My Heart*, and *Surrender My Heart*, which follows a family of three women who must confront the past to find redemption and second chances. She's also the author of the epic fantasy romance series, *The Angelorum Twelve Chronicles*. L.G. enjoys connecting with readers at book clubs and reader events.

If you enjoyed this book, (please!) leave a **REVIEW or RATING** on **Amazon, Bookbub, Goodreads, #BookTok**, or wherever you purchased the book.

Find/Follow L.G.:

Website & Newsletter www.lgoconnor.com
Bookbub @LGOConnor for New Releases
Substack (@lgoconnor) for her Wellness and Writerly posts

Acknowledgments

Thank you to my tremendous team for all your love and support. Without you, the final book wouldn't have been what it is today. Thank you to my "cross-stitch" beta reading crew: Marilyn, Lesley, and Eileen; the expanded beta reading team: Wendy, West, and Phoebe; my editor, Ray Rhamey; and the final pair of eyes, Nancee Adams-Taylor. Without them, this book wouldn't have been nearly as good.